Pure Sin
Partners in Passion

Sahara Kelly
S.L. Carpenter

Ellora's Cave
Romantica Publishing

What the critics are saying...

❧

5 Hearts "To choose any or all of the *Partners in Passion* books is a gift to reader's senses with the author's use of pages of delectable detail. The love scenes go on for pages and build to an exuberant climax. Each story has fun characters that draw on their own insecurities." ~ *Night Owl Romance Reviews*

4.5 Stars "*Pure Sin* is a wonderfully written story of two people who find each other and fall in love through sexual exploration and discovery. The story itself is funny, sexy, interesting, heartwarming and will leave you with a smile on your face and your juices flowing. […] *Pure Sin* is not just a sexy love story but is funny with many twists and turns. […] I highly recommend this book to anyone and applaud SL Carpenter & Sahara Kelly for the duo's great book and wonderful talent." ~ *Two Lips Reviews*

An Ellora's Cave Romantica Publication

www.ellorascave.com

Pure Sin

ISBN 9781419957444
ALL RIGHTS RESERVED.
Pure Sin Copyright © 2007 Sahara Kelly and S.L. Carpenter
Edited by Briana St. James.
Cover art by Syneca.
Photo courtesy S.L. Carpenter.

This book printed in the U.S.A. by Jasmine-Jade Enterprises, LLC.

Electronic book Publication January 2007
Trade paperback Publication March 2008

With the exception of quotes used in reviews, this book may not be reproduced or used in whole or in part by any means existing without written permission from the publisher, Ellora's Cave Publishing, Inc.® 1056 Home Avenue, Akron OH 44310-3502.

Warning: The unauthorized reproduction or distribution of this copyrighted work is illegal. Criminal copyright infringement, including infringement without monetary gain, is investigated by the FBI and is punishable by up to 5 years in federal prison and a fine of $250,000.
(http://www.fbi.gov/ipr/)

This book is a work of fiction and any resemblance to persons, living or dead, or places, events or locales is purely coincidental. The characters are productions of the authors' imagination and used fictitiously.

Also by Sahara Kelly

A Kink in Her Tails
Anasazi Lassie
An Unkindness of Ravens
A Siege of Herons
At Cross Purposes
A Watch of Nightingales
Beating Level Nine
By Shadows Bound
Detour *with S.L. Carpenter*
Ellora's Cavemen: Dreams of the Oasis II *(anthology)*
Ellora's Cavemen: Legendary Tails III *(anthology)*
Ellora's Cavemen: Tales from the Temple I *(anthology)*
Flame of Shadows
For Research Purposes Only
Game Over
Georgie and Her Dragon
Guardians of Time 1: Alana's Magic Lamp
Guardians of Time 2: Finding the Zero-G Spot
Guardians of Time 3: Peta and the Wolfe
Hansell and Gretty
Haunting Love Alley *with S.L. Carpenter*
Irish Enchantment *(anthology)*
Knights Elemental
Lyndhurst and Lydia
Madam Charlie
Magnus Ravynne and Mistress Swann
Mystic Visions *(anthology)*
Partners in Passion 1: Eleanor and Justin
Partners in Passion 2: No Limits
Perfect Whore
Persephone's Wings
Scars of the Lash
Scars of the Soul

Shadows of Therese
Sir Philip Ashton's Eyes
Sizzle
The Glass Stripper
The Gypsy Lovers
The Sun God's Woman
Tales of the Beau Monde 1: Inside Lady Miranda
Tales of the Beau Monde 2: Miss Beatrice's Bottom
Tales of the Beau Monde 3: Lying With Louisa
Tales of the Beau Monde 4: Pleasuring Miss Poppy
Wingin' It

Also by S.L. Carpenter

Betty and the Beast
Broken
Dark Lord Origins
Dark Lust
Detour *with Sahara Kelly*
Haunting Love Alley
In the End
Learning to Live Again
More Lust
Naked Lust
Partners in Passion 1: Eleanor and Justin *with Sahara Kelly*
Partners in Passion 2: No Limits *with Sahara Kelly*
Slippery When Wet
Strange Lust
Toys 4 Us

About the Authors

Sahara Kelly was transplanted from old England to New England where she now lives with her husband and teenage son. Making the transition from her historical regency novels to Romantica™ has been surprisingly easy, and now Sahara can't imagine writing anything else. She is dedicated to the premise that everybody should have fantasies.

S.L. Carpenter is a born and raised California man. He does both writing and cover art for novels as outlets for his overactive libido and twisted mind. His inspiration is his wife, who keeps him well trained. Writing is his true joy. It gives him freedom and expression for both his sensual and humorous sides.

Sahara and S.L. welcome comments from readers. You can find their websites and email addresses on their author bio pages at www.ellorascave.com.

Tell Us What You Think
We appreciate hearing reader opinions about our books. You can email us at Comments@EllorasCave.com.

PURE SIN
ಸು

Dedication

~

To all the readers who made no secret of how much they liked the first two novels in the Partners in Passion series, Scott and Sahara would like to say thank you by dedicating this story to them. Without such support and encouragement, this book might not have been written. Well, it probably would have been written, but we'd call it something else.

Trademarks Acknowledgement

~

The author acknowledges the trademarked status and trademark owners of the following wordmarks mentioned in this work of fiction:

Axminster: Crossley Axminster, Inc.

Harley-Davidson: H-D Michigan, Inc.

Lexus: Toyota Motor Corporation, Japan

Smurfs: Studio Peyo, S.A. Corporation, Switzerland

Viagra: Pfizer Inc. Corporation Delaware, New York

Prologue

Amy's eyes began to water behind the blindfold as the salt from her sweat burned them and bright lights shone on her, making everything hot. She was intensely aroused and gasping as the low hum began again. "No, Mike—no more—please, not again."

Mike clicked the controller in his hand, making her groan. She wiggled her ass on the black leather device below her splayed thighs, knowing her body was being willingly used once more. She was weakening and yet when Mike tugged on the rope in his hand, she let the leather cuffs on her wrists pull her body upward, her breasts thrusting toward him. She was naked, exposed and wet with excitement.

"*Fuck it,* Amy. Fuck it like it was my cock." Mike sounded wicked, a menacing presence in the shadows.

There was a constant clicking—a sound that jolted Amy back from the brink of her exhaustion. She rocked back and forth, riding the piece of leather-covered equipment with a mixture of pleasure and apprehension. Each time Mike pulled on the rope she rose, letting the long pink dildo slide out of her dripping cunt. Firmly fixed to the stool, it hummed as it awaited her descent.

Amy trembled as she felt Mike fondle her breast. Her nipples were hard and super sensitive to his touch.

"Damn—you are *so* fucking *hot*. I love controlling you." He flicked her nipple with his thumb, causing Amy to quiver, then leaned close to let his tongue roll over the tight tip.

Amy moaned and tried to push her breast against his mouth.

"Uh uh. Remember who's in charge here. Don't make me punish you." The controller in his hand changed its sound from a low hum to a thrumming pulse.

Amy's mouth dropped open and she threw her head back. The dildo began to churn inside her cunt but she couldn't lower her body fully onto it because her arms were still pulled upward. The opening of her pussy was being stretched and massaged.

Her mind raced for a grip on reality — she'd agreed to this. She had agreed to let Mike own her — control her — to let him rule her sexually. To surrender to him completely.

A loud click distracted her from her daze just as Mike released the rope. Her weakened legs let her torso fall onto the dildo, embedding it deep into her pussy, and Amy knew it wouldn't be long now as the steady pulse rubbed along her inner walls. Her arms ached, her legs were sore and her entire body shuddered, spent and wet with perspiration.

But still Mike wasn't done.

"*Ammyyyy*, are you still with me? I have something for you." Mike's voice echoed in her fogged mind. She felt him close — felt him touch her cheek as he stood before her.

The slow, rhythmic grind of the dildo continued to cause Amy such deep pleasure that it was almost impossible to focus on what he was saying. Her mind drifted this way and that, at sea on great rolling waves of ecstasy that robbed her of conscious thought.

"I want you to do something for me, Amy. Are you listening?"

"Yes, Mike." She heard him through a fog — a mist of desire that held her trapped and barely functioning.

He lifted her head, making her sit upright.

There was a familiar metallic rasp — so familiar that both her pussy and her mouth responded. The juices from her cunt flowed along her inner thighs as she waited patiently now, licking her lips, knowing what was coming next.

Sure enough, Amy felt the smooth head of Mike's cock as it brushed against her mouth. She opened it slightly, letting the heat from inside escape. He teased her, rubbing her cheeks with the swollen head of his cock.

"You know what I want, Amy. You *know*."

He moved forward, the heat from his body dusting her face with fire. She wondered if he was looking down at her, then she heard him grab his thickened cock, the slight sound of flesh on flesh unmistakable.

She waited, knowing he would move, knowing he would press himself against her lips.

He did.

Willingly, Amy parted them and he slid into her welcoming wet mouth. Mike let out the sigh that always told her he was entering heaven. She traced the vein along the base of his cock with her tongue, loving the way he moved his hips slowly back and forth, fucking her mouth. She couldn't hold back the soft moans that she could feel vibrating through their joined bodies and along his spine.

Like distant fireworks, the odd clicking noise continued, but Amy barely heard it as a rush of pleasure billowed up inside her. Finding her rhythm, she sucked on Mike's cock and fucked the dildo buried inside her cunt—each a counterpoint to the other.

He stroked his large cock into her mouth as Amy stroked the large rubber cock below her. She wanted to make Mike come and she desperately wanted to come with him—to give him the gift of sharing their orgasms. She sucked and licked his cock, savoring it, loving the fact that he moaned as she slurped loudly around the engorged head.

Her arms burned from the strain of being stretched unnaturally above her but she didn't care—it had begun. She was climaxing and nothing mattered now but the bliss of her own ecstasy.

She barely felt Mike grab the back of her head and force his cock deeper into her mouth, hard, throbbing and ready to explode. Pulling back, she dragged her teeth along the swollen vein on his cock. Plunging back into her mouth, Mike groaned, grabbed a fistful of Amy's hair in his hand—and erupted.

Her entire body shuddered and shook as she peaked and moaned sounds that had no meaning. Streams of juices flowed from her cunt, soaking her thighs and the stool as tears of pleasure fell over her face, splashing their way down to join the moisture wetting her legs.

Afloat on a gale of sensation, all she could hear were the little clicking fireworks. She never noticed the flash of bright light accompanying them.

Pure Sin

Chapter One
ಸು

She was *coming*.

No two ways about it, the woman in the photograph was *orgasming*, right there—front and center—in beautifully shadowed black and white glory.

Tracy Harmon blinked and swallowed as she looked at the large, gorgeously lit image dominating the far wall of the gallery.

This was truly a wonderful centerpiece to the exhibit—a moment in time captured for eternity. The ultimate achievement of male and female, yet here there was the added twist of bondage and a dominant male clearly fucking the woman's mouth with great enthusiasm.

Muscles were ripped from their channels of flesh to stand free and hard, casting rigid shadows upon dewy skin. Bodies arched, necks contorted—it was a poem to ecstasy and bondage and it held Tracy rapt and unmoving as she absorbed the savage beauty of the scene.

It was almost overwhelming. The slick, shiny leather between the woman's thighs testified to her arousal as clearly as her nipples, hard buds thrusting toward the man dominating her. Tracy guessed there was a device—a dildo or vibrator perhaps—within the woman, since she'd seen a seat like that on-line at one of the fetish auction sites when she'd dropped by recently.

Unbidden, a lick of heat touched Tracy's belly—a quiet ember of lust, of hunger—a suppressed desire to experience the kind of passion she could see on the woman's face.

"Jesus. Now *that's* something I wouldn't want on my office wall."

Tracy jumped, jerked from her private contemplation by the smoothly practiced voice of her date Simon Travers.

"Really?" It was all she could think of to say. She honestly hadn't heard what he'd muttered. Something that was happening more and more these days.

"Well, good God, Trace. Look at that. Raw, rough—nothing attractive about that whatsoever. I mean sex is sex, but does it have to be shown in all its gritty and messy realism?"

Tracy shook her head. "You're wrong, Simon. Quite wrong. This is—beautiful."

He snorted. "Well, I guess we have different definitions of that word. I mean *really*…" He moved closer, hand to his chin, assuming the classic pose of art critic and sophisticated enthusiast.

Neither of which, in Tracy's opinion, he was.

"Look, her body's all wrong. Small breasts, nipples too large, completely out of proportion. She's got what could be a birthmark or something here, just below her waist—why they didn't brush that out I'll never understand—and just look at that hair between her legs. How *provincial*." He curled his lip and stepped backward. "Now if you're looking for something more along the lines of *art*, I suggest any of these over here…"

As Tracy could have predicted, Simon dragged her back to the room housing the familiar leather and studs shots—busty women who looked like they had just come from makeup and wardrobe smiling glassily over leather whips while poised on massively spiked and booted heels.

They were unremarkable, unstimulating, unartistic to her eyes and generally falling into the category of "blah". Which, come to think of it, was just about where Simon himself was in her life.

Fortunately, his cell phone rang—again—and while he took the call, Tracy took the opportunity to leave his side.

The relief that poured over her as she made her way back to the center of the gallery was almost palpable. This would be absolutely the *very* last night she had anything to do with Simon Travers. Bringing him was a mistake, but the invitation to attend this opening had come while they were still in the hot-and-heavy stage of new lovers.

That had lasted all of a week. Simon seemed to love the thrill of the chase, but once the prey was captured…well, the bloom fell off the rose pretty damn quickly. Sadly boredom had followed them to bed, Simon's lovemaking being uninspired and Tracy's responses borderline comatose.

He was good to look at but—like his job—pretty much a flash in the pan, a firework that exploded in glory but faded to nothing within seconds. He'd never really sent Tracy into orbit the way her women's magazines told her the *right* lover was supposed to.

She walked back through the politely muttering crowd to look once more at the striking image that had grabbed her by the throat.

That's what I want.

The unrestrained wildness she could see in the posture of the woman coming in the photo.

The passion barely contained in her body, the eagerness with which her cheeks hollowed around her lover's cock, the blindfold hiding what must have been eyes shining with desire.

That's what I want.

The surrender she'd offered to her man, the control she'd willingly given up. Her arms could not move, her mouth was filled, her body plundered from beneath—and yet through it all there was a sense of joy. Of wondrous pleasures experienced by both.

That's what I want.

To submit. To pass over all responsibility for sex to someone who would take it for the gift it surely was. To follow instructions, walk a guided path to pleasure led by a firm hand, to relinquish the need to meet thrust with thrust, to drive in tandem with a lover.

That was fine in its way, but Tracy knew that there had to be more. The deeply hidden urge to surrender herself to the hands of a skilled and dominating lover surfaced for a few brief moments as she looked at the images of women and men doing just that.

That's what I want.

Uncomfortably aware of heat rising through her breasts and moisture beginning to dampen her panties, Tracy sighed and turned away.

Only to find her gaze held fast by another pair of eyes.

He was watching her face like it was the only face in the room.

For a few moments the world blurred around Tracy, sounds fading, people dropping out of focus. It was as if there were only the two of them left—a man and a woman standing, looking at each other.

A part of her brain registered the usual checkpoints. He was about six foot or so, not overly muscled but certainly solid in all the right places. He probably jogged or at least had an active health club membership.

His eyes were brown, a dark brown, not the gold-flecked variety that she saw in her own mirror every day. No, his were more the brown of rich Swiss chocolate. Tracy licked her lips although whether at the thought of chocolate or this man she wasn't sure.

His suit was well-cut and appropriate, but he didn't look *at home* in it. Not a man who wore one on a daily basis, that was for sure. Tracy's gaze took all this information in and her brain processed it, but elsewhere in her head she saw him in jeans and a T-shirt, possibly riding a horse or something.

And then she saw him in nothing at all—riding *her.*

Her throat closed up as she swam into visions of incredibly erotic sex with this total stranger. Him holding her down, hands stretched high past her head, doing wonderfully dominating things to her body.

Blindfolding her, restraining her, fucking her until there was no breath left in her body and yet she would still cry out for more...

That's what I want.

With a gasp she wrenched her mind away from the lurid scene, hoping that nobody would *ever* know what she'd just imagined. She blinked just as the man did something quite out of character for an art enthusiast.

* * * * *

George stood motionless, his mind filled with visions of action. Here he was at an erotic art show on a Monday night. Images of sex, dominance and submission surrounded him. People of all shapes and sizes circled the art gallery but George stood without moving in the center of the room.

Something had his undivided attention. *Something* had grabbed him and kept him captive. His eyes stared but he saw nothing. For a single moment he found a sense of peace. A smile crossed his face, then he yelled "*touchdown...yesssss*". He pumped his fist by his side.

He pulled the earplug from his ear and felt his face burn as people glanced curiously at him. With an embarrassed whistle he headed into a nearby corner, never noticing the woman who had returned his stare, or the fact that she'd not moved after taking one look into his eyes.

He'd also missed her muffled laugh as he cheered the touchdown and the way she held in her amusement by biting her bottom lip—hard. She'd turned away then, so that even if he'd looked for her, all he'd have seen would have been the back of her head.

George wandered past the outer walls of the gallery, trying to blend in with the art-lovers but knowing that in reality he got better reception from his cell service there. He was all slicked up in a suit—which he hated—and listening to the game was about the only bright spot in his evening.

He caught a glimpse of himself reflected off a framed and matted photo. His short dark hair definitely gave him the look of a secret agent or spy. Definitely Double-O. Licensed to kill. His name? Cluny…George Cluny.

"Oh *here* you are." A breathy voice broke into George's peaceful realm. His team had the ball on the seventeen-yard line too. He sighed.

He'd let Tina drag him to this gallery and this exhibit. He would have been totally comfortable staying home and watching football, drinking a few beers, jogging on his treadmill and perhaps getting a blowjob before bed.

But Tina had other plans. She was a *mingler*, someone George regarded as not too distantly related to a leech. She sucked all the self-gratifying praise out of a social situation and did as much ass-kissing at the same time as humanly possible. Everybody knew somebody like that—George, unfortunately, was *dating* one.

He cared for her but the relationship was high-maintenance and had taken a strange turn about a year ago. The woman he'd had fun with became a human doll. She had breast implants, facial injections and was suddenly more worried about her social calendar than her dating obligations. He had to make an appointment to have sex and she'd only schedule him for an hour or so a week, unless there was a program about beauty aids on cable TV. *Then* it was twenty minutes—if he was lucky. She opened a little boutique with money she borrowed from George and, in his opinion, mutated into some kind of a female Frankenstein.

This little artistic excursion was solely so that she could make contacts. George looked at most of the art as basically boring—nothing struck him as attention-grabbing or really defining *art* in his mind.

"You embarrassed me, George. Yelling in the room like that. Put that radio or whatever away. There are some people I want you to meet. They could really help the boutique's business." Tina brushed at his suit as she frowned at him. She licked her fingertips and smoothed George's hair behind his ear.

"Tina, for God's sake. My *mom* used to do that and I hated it even then. Stop treating me like a child." Irritated, George rolled his eyes, but as he'd expected, his protests were ignored. She pulled him by the hand and they walked into the eye of the storm.

Fifteen minutes later, George had squirmed his way out of the crowd. "Free at last." He'd turned away from the loudest and busiest group to find some space of his own. As he did so, he bumped into a very attractive woman. He blinked a few times, stunned and dumbfounded as his gut churned unexpectedly. "Um…uhh…"

She was looking at the photo of the couple that had caught his attention too.

"Did your guys win?" She didn't turn around to look at him, just spoke over her shoulder.

"I was going to check." He grinned. At least somebody didn't mind if he kept tabs on his team. He followed her gaze once more. "Now *that's* a picture!" George stared at the black and white image.

She nodded. "Isn't it gorgeous? Look at the shadowing, the textures…"

"The woman's body…" George continued her train of thought almost without realizing it. He glanced down at her, noticing her eyes, transfixed by the photograph and glimmering as she stared at it. They were a sort of warm brown but there were also gold flecks catching the lighting and sparkling as she flashed a quick look at him. She was breathing like she'd just dashed across the street and there was a hint of perspiration across her chest.

This woman is hot.

It was a nice chest too. What he could see of it, anyway. She had on a shirt in rich colors that went well with the thick dark hair coiled at her neck. Something soft and green swathed her arms and hugged her body. Rather like George would if he had half the chance.

"You like this picture?" He politely asked the question, although he already knew the answer. He wanted to hear her speak—keep her talking.

"It's not a picture…it's *art*. There's something about it. Passion, lust, emotions, I can't describe it, but whatever it is it's just fucking *hot*." She blushed. "God, sorry. I'm not usually so foul mouthed. Tracy. Tracy Harmon." She extended her hand toward George.

"Cluny…George Cluny." The perfect timing for his line.

"Does that line work with women?" Eyebrow raised in disbelief, Tracy was a brick wall that his charm bounced uselessly against, even though her palm was burning hot against his.

"Uhh, obviously not."

"*George Clooney*?" She tipped her head to one side.

George raised one hand and stopped her. "That's Cluny with a *u* like the museum, not two *o*'s like the guy in the movies. It's a curse I suffer every day, but I have to admit it's great for getting dinner reservations."

She shared his grin as they both turned and looked at the photo again. "I believe it."

Her fragrance wafted through the space between them and suddenly the lights dimmed for George. His heart thudded as his nose inhaled something delicately feminine, making him think of silk sheets, soft thighs and pussy.

He wasn't a man who had visions, but he was getting one now. This woman, naked, beneath him—staring at him from those big brown eyes as he held her immobile and plunged deeply into her cunt.

He gulped down a big lump of lust, fought another big lump that threatened to distort his trousers and tried to focus on something else. His team. Tina. Oh *shit…Tina.*

His budding hard-on immediately withered to his mingled disappointment and relief. He was able to jerk his brains back to the picture in front of them.

George narrowed his eyes and leaned near one corner. "Son of a bitch. *Marcus* took this photo." He shook his head. "Well, I'll be damned."

"Who?" Tracy looked at him curiously.

"See the tag? *Not for Sale.* Photographer…*Marcus.* I *know* this guy if it's the one I'm thinking of. I did some website stuff for him and his wife a while back. She was this hotshot model and he'd taken some great photos. Didn't know he was still into this after everything that happened."

"What happened?"

"Well, he…oh *shit.*" George stopped talking.

"What are you doing over here, George?" Tina glared at Tracy and put her hand on her hip. "And this is…?" She motioned toward Tracy.

"Sorry. Tracy Harmon, this is um…"

"Tina R. I own the Tina R Boutique on Elm Street. I'm sure you've heard of the place." With a disapproving frown she looked at the picture then back at Tracy, eyeing her up and down. "Although I don't think you shop there." Having dissed Tracy's clothes very smoothly, she tipped her chin at George. "Come on, George, we need to go before everyone else leaves."

"Nice to meet you, Tracy. Look…if you ever need a website or anything…" He handed Tracy his card and took a last long look into her whiskey brown eyes.

Yowsa!

Chapter Two

ඟ

"Honestly, Simon? I don't give a shit."

Tracy held her cell phone away from her ear to avoid having her eardrums blasted by a bellow of wounded male pride.

It was the last conversation, the last straw, the camel's back was about to break…it was the penultimate moment in their relationship and the ultimate was about to occur.

"Simon. *Fuck off*. We're through. Done. Finito. You know it and I know it. It's been fun. It's over. Take me off your speed dial. You're already off mine. Goodbye."

She snapped the tiny unit closed and tossed it onto her desk where it settled comfortably on a pile of papers and letters Tracy had been sorting through before the unpleasantness began.

She and Simon had been doomed from the start. Different tastes, different friends, different goals—other than a few nice sessions in bed there had been little between them other than a similarity in lifestyles. They both worked hard and were devoted to their businesses.

Simon made a lot of money from his—Tracy derived a lot of satisfaction from hers. And sometimes enough money to splurge on good shoes. Which were, all things considered, a better investment than Simon.

She shrugged off a momentary depression. Her days were filled with work, phone calls, occasional get-togethers with friends and the challenge of meeting her clients' visions. It was fun and mostly fulfilling.

But more and more she was getting a niggling little feeling behind one ear that there should be something else — that there was a place in her universe she was seriously ignoring. That as the big three-oh loomed in the windshield of her future she was driving toward it down a rather empty road, alone in the low-slung sports car of her nicely equipped life.

Okay — too many automotive ads this month.

Tracy grinned at herself and shook her head, reaching for the pile of paperwork once more. For somebody who ran an Internet ad consultancy she still seemed to have a shitload of the stuff.

A loud ring made her jump and for a second she stared at her cell phone, wondering if it was Simon. Then it blared again and she realized it was her real, actual desk phone — ringing its head off. Something that rarely happened.

Tentatively she lifted the receiver. "Harmon Consultants. Tracy Harmon speaking."

"Hey, Tracy honey. Good to hear your voice. It's Eleanor."

Tracy's jaw dropped. "Ohmigod. *Eleanor*? I don't believe it. Shit, you damn near made me wet my panties by calling on this phone, you crazy woman. Why didn't you email me? Or call my cell like everybody else? God, how are you? It's been *years*…you still married to Mister Superhunk?"

A husky laugh sounded in Tracy's ears as she paused for breath. "If you'd just shut up for a minute I'd answer all those questions and more."

"Sorry." Tracy giggled. "Just hearing from you is a fabulous high, sweetie."

"Sounds like you needed one."

"Got that right. Your timing is perfect." Tracy leaned back in her chair and ignored the work in front of her as she gazed at the ceiling and talked to her old friend. "So what's cooking in your neck of the woods?"

"Not much. I was just thinking about us in college, laughing at the memories, and I thought well hell, *call* the girl and laugh *with* her."

"They were good times, huh?"

"Some of 'em, yeah. Of course, knowing what I know now, they could've been a helluva lot better." Eleanor snickered.

"Having seen your hubby, I can imagine. How's he doing? How's the bar?"

"Justin's fine. The bar is doing great business and so's the restaurant next door. I told you my sister's running it, didn't I?"

Tracy nodded into the phone, remembering Eleanor talking about her sister Jodi. "Yes, you did. Glad it's doing well."

"You know, I've got an idea…"

Tracy snorted. "Uh oh. When you used to say that it meant trouble. Or an all-night study session."

Eleanor laughed. "Not this time. You still have your ad consulting business, right?"

"Yes, why?"

"*Weeelllll…*"

Eleanor's drawn out word slithered into Tracy's ear, making her wriggle. "Spit it out, my friend. You'll bust something trying to be subtle."

"Okay."

Tracy could hear Eleanor's indrawn breath. *Here it comes.*

"This guy who works at the bar, Mike, is thinking of buying into a small inn near here. Thing is, with places like that, you have to draw the customers, create a market for yourself, or there's zippo in the way of income."

Tracy nodded. She and Eleanor had met in Introductory Business 101 and remained friends ever since. The skills they'd learned had stayed with them as well, even though Eleanor's now focused on the bar and restaurant she'd married into when she made an honest man of Justin Collins.

"So we've been batting around ideas here and Justin suggested Mike should think about using the Internet. With all the travel services out there a small country inn seems a natural addition to some of their offerings. The more exclusive ones who can suggest a romantic weekend for two or something."

Tracy was silent for a moment, her brain skittering around the potentials and the possibilities.

"Hmm." She stared absently at the wall across from her desk. "Got anything around there that would help sell it?"

This time the silence was on Eleanor's end of the conversation. Then she spoke. "Look, why don't you come visit? See the place? Take a little time off from your desktop system and your monitor, pack your laptop and come see us?"

Tracy blinked. "Come stay with you?"

"Well, I was actually thinking of your staying at the inn itself. It's still running, got a few devoted employees who keep things functioning and a manager older than dirt. Just so you can get a feel for the place. I'd say stay with us but things are a bit chaotic at the moment…"

"You moved into a house recently, didn't you?"

"Yeah. We needed the space but there's a bit of remodeling to do and we don't exactly have all the time in the world to do it."

"Why? I thought these things were supposed to evolve naturally…" Tracy frowned.

"They do. Unfortunately, so does the human race."

"Huh?"

"We've got about four and a half months to get this particular project finished before our *personal* project arrives."

"*Ohmigod.*" Tracy nearly fell off her chair as she squealed into the phone. "*Ohmigod ohmigod ohmigod. You're pregnant?*"

Eleanor giggled again. "Yep. Big as a house already. Ready for peppermint stick ice-cream by the gallon, lost my ankles two weeks ago and still waiting for the morning sickness thing. Doesn't look like it's going to hit me."

Tracy shook her head. "I can't believe it. Congratulations, honey. I'm sooooo thrilled."

"Yeah, me too. Most of the time. So you see with the nursery and stuff…"

"God yeah, I understand. No problem. And I'd *love* to come visit with you and Justin."

"You just want to watch me waddle." Eleanor sounded wistful. "I waddle, you know."

"I'm sure you waddle better than any mom-to-be has ever waddled before. And I'm sure Justin loves you anyway, waddle and all."

Eleanor laughed loud. "Oh God, I miss you. When can you get here? And don't make me laugh again or I'll wet my panties…"

Thoughts of this particular conversation brought a huge smile to Tracy's face in the following days as she prepared to head out of town and see her old friend. She was still smiling as she drove into the countryside and left her business suits behind along with a lot of other baggage she didn't need.

The sun was shining, the leaves were just starting to turn to gold and red and amber—it was a perfect day to shake off the pressures of her life and just *breathe*. The further away from town she got, the lighter the air felt around her and the less she worried about the appointments she'd cancelled or the video conferences she'd rescheduled.

Her business was in good shape, she didn't have much in the way of outstanding debts and she answered to nobody but herself and her clients. It was a heavy responsibility at times—being in total control of one's own life—but it was the road she'd chosen.

Pure Sin

Tracy followed the highway for a couple of hours then hit her signal for the turnoff to Eleanor's. She had been there before, for their wedding, but it had been a while so she slowed down, making sure she remembered the route.

Justin's bar was charming—exactly what she'd expected to find in a small town tucked into the countryside. It was warm and welcoming, offering music, the occasional karaoke night, dancing and now apparently a good meal next door.

The local economy was pretty strong thanks to a couple of agricultural companies specializing in organic products and research, and the demographics featured more in the way of college-educated twenty-five- to forty-five-year-olds than one would expect in such a rural community. There was even a little vineyard and local winery, making use of the shorter growing season to produce a quite tasty white wine.

Tracy's heart jumped happily at the thought of sharing a glass with Eleanor. This was such a damn *good* idea she had no clue why she hadn't done it before. It was time to shed the corporate skin, drop the rigorously controlled businesswoman and just have *fun*. Of course, come to think of it, Eleanor probably couldn't drink.

Oh well, Tracy would just have to drink enough for both of them.

With that delightful thought uppermost in her mind, Tracy pointed her car in the direction of Eleanor, Justin and "The Mating Place".

* * * * *

The darkness shattered like glass. Bright flashes ripping through the shadows, over and over. The image etched itself in George's mind as if he was there. He *was* there—in his fantasy.

The picture from the gallery took on a new perspective. *He* was the man controlling the woman. *He* had the power to release her. The heat in his body rose to a scorching level as the blood pumped in his veins faster and harder. He could feel his heart pounding in the core of his chest.

George looked down as the woman slid her mouth free of his swollen cock.

When their gazes collided, George nearly jumped—it was Tracy Harmon's face he saw in his fantasy. Not the girl in the photo.

Waking from his dream, George rolled over in his bed. The blankets were propped up like a tent, with his cock a very effective center pole. This had been a good dream. It was also a moment where George regretted his split with Tina. One of her surgeries—the one putting collagen in her lips—had truly added a new dimension to her oral capabilities.

But inevitably they had broken up for the final time. Her self-absorbed personality was too overwhelming and she was dragging him into this unrealistic view she had on life and relationships. He refused to be a figurine in her dream world anymore. George Cluny wanted to be something else. Something more important.

George sat up. He was alone, horny, had a massive hard-on and was hungry. All the makings of a porn-filled, late night-early morning session of *hand-to-gland* love.

He leaned over to open his secret drawer stash of nighttime necessities. The potato chips and warm soda were in the bottom drawer next to the condoms and the motion lotion. He was prepared for anything.

George wasn't a porn connoisseur but he knew what he liked. The threesomes with a guy becoming a "manwich" between two girls were appealing. The storylines were optional but the sex was a must. Especially the controlling-type sex. Movies where the man had complete control over his woman. Hands bound, body exposed, nipples hard and a cunt so sweltering hot that a man could melt just fucking her. Pure uninhibited offering of what a man demands.

His sex life with Tina had been more a job than a pleasure. She wouldn't let him pull her hair because her curls wouldn't stay in for long. And anyway the stuff she used to get and keep her tumble of curls smelled like shit on his hands.

The only control he experienced was her telling him the correct position for their sex and how long they had. Oh sure, they started out great. She was a typical college graduate nymphet and her infatuation with oral sex sealed the deal for George. Tina could suck start a leaf blower—she even showed George once. After she'd gone down on him, he swore his balls had been sucked out through his cock.

But people change. They both did. She found a career and success in her own way while George was content to let success find him. He was incredibly lucky as well, figuring his achievements were due as much to chance as they were to his strong business intuition.

Looking up at his flat-screen TV on the bedroom wall, George sighed as he saw the enormous painting Tina had commissioned dominating the rest of the wall space. It was a portrait of her and clearly indicated her egocentric way of being the apex of George's world.

But no more.

As George stared reflectively at the detail of the picture, he realized something. He remembered how much it had cost him to get the painting done and how long it had taken. Now he knew exactly what he wanted to replace it above his TV.

That photograph. The one taken by his old friend Marcus.

The one he'd seen in the gallery the night he'd met Tracy Harmon.

* * * * *

After fruitlessly searching through old phone numbers, calling the art gallery and finally promising a fifty-dollar bribe to a hungry student assistant, George got Marcus' address. He decided it was a good time to take a vacation so he notified his office that he'd be back in a week or so. He didn't need to be there anyway. It was a tightly run company and he'd hired top-notch people for his sales and distribution fields. Strictly speaking, his presence wasn't even necessary. He was just a poster boy for the business, but it had his name on it and he liked being around his employees.

So for once he took advantage of his position, hopped in his car and headed west. Being a typical male, he swore off asking for directions and promptly got lost. He also refused to admit that as night crept closer he was a little nervous about his body ending up in a ditch somewhere after being killed by a stalker or chainsaw-wielding maniac.

Too many horror movies from the video rental store.

Before he had chance to totally freak himself out, he saw the lights of a small town glowing in the distance. It took no time at all to find himself back in civilization. And conveniently outside the very place he wanted to be.

The Mating Place.

As the bar door swung open, a cloud of smoke and noise bellowed out. "Ahh, my kind of place." George smiled as he walked in. It was the kind of establishment that had its own life…people were laughing, talking in groups and there was a strong feel of fun in the air.

George walked straight to the bar and caught the eye of the tall, good-looking bartender, who raised his hand in the universal gesture that says *I'll be right over…*

The delay was caused by several women giggling and flirting with him. *Lucky guy.*

"Sorry, I had a bet with the girls and had to make sure they paid up. What'll you have?"

George glanced back down at the women who were muttering amongst themselves. "Must have been a good bet. I haven't seen women that flustered in a while."

The bartender grinned. "They were all betting each other that I'd go home with one of them. All I had to do was to mention my wife and the conversation ended pretty quickly. A few years back though…mmm. *Smorgasbord*."

George dug for his wallet. "I'll have a whiskey with a beer chaser. I'll pass on the draft…give me a nice German one if you got it." He looked at the nametag dangling from the bartender's shirt pocket…*Justin*. "Is Marcus around? I heard he works here and I'm trying to get in touch with him."

"Yep, he works here—for me, as a matter of fact. He's away right now, though, with Jodi. He'll be back in a few days." With a quick flick of the cap the mug was filled with cool fragrant beer and the shot glass topped off with a richly glowing whiskey that was, as Justin promised, *the good stuff*.

"Jodi? Who's she?" George downed the whiskey shot. His eyes blurred with a glisten of moisture from the alcohol and he gasped. "Wow, that's some *good* shit." Quickly, a gulp of beer followed the whiskey down George's burning throat.

"That's his business and I don't discuss my friends with strangers. His personal life is just that. Personal." Justin turned to clean off the stray beer bottles and glasses from the bar.

George sighed, realizing how vague he'd sounded. "I apologize. I'm an old friend of his. My name is George Cluny." Justin looked up, as did the few remaining girls at the end of the bar.

"George Clooney?"

"Cluny. C-L-U-N-Y." He shrugged as the girls went back to their conversation, losing interest in him once he spelled his name. "That happens a lot." He shook his head and sipped from the beer again.

Justin leaned on the bar, looking thoughtful. "You know…I think I remember Marcus talking about you. Something about a website and stuff for his ex?"

"Yeah, she was one hot woman. Although—and he probably wouldn't mind me saying so—she was kind of a bitch too. Anyway I just wanted to see him. Had a business proposition for him."

"You can't take him away from here. He's my best bartender and I don't want to deal with my wife bitching at me all the time because I'd have to cover his shifts." Justin laughed with George as they shared a male moment, both understanding the fear of a woman's wrath.

"Nothing like that," George reassured Justin. "I just want to buy one of his pictures and catch up on old times. Plus I needed a break from the city hustle. Seemed like a good chance to do both."

Justin shrugged. "There's not a lot to do around this town. We need to get a baseball or football team closer. Marcus will be back in a few days, I think."

"Well, I guess I'll just hang around for a while. Wait for him to get back." He looked back along the bar to the ladies at the other end. "Maybe see if I can get some company for a night or two. Can you recommend a place to stay?"

Looking around him absently, Justin pursed his lips in thought. "Hmm. Back down the highway—maybe twenty miles or so—is your standard hotel. But Purett's Inn is a lot closer…down this street until it dead-ends and hang a left. Maybe fifteen minutes." Justin gestured with his hands. "Nice old place. They're renovating a bit and it could use more work, but at least it's quiet. Tell the owners you know me…they'll hook you up. They still owe me some money on a bar tab. Ol' Monty likes his brandy. He has a special blend that I get for him and it's *really good* shit."

"Sounds good to me. I need someplace with a bit of character. I can't stand those roadside motels. Too noisy and crowded with kids screaming up and down the halls. Thanks, Justin. I'm sure I'll be around again. You've got a nice place here." George pulled out a couple of bills and tossed them on the bar to cover his drinks.

Justin nodded his thanks. "You'll have to try the food next door. Great muffs. Er…I mean *muffins*. I have muff on the brain tonight."

George laughed and left the bar. It was getting late and he wanted nothing more than a quiet room and at least ten hours of uninterrupted sleep.

That would be pure heaven.

Chapter Three

൩

Tracy squinted into the dusk, looking for road signs as she tried to follow Eleanor's directions. She'd found Eleanor's house with no problems, but she'd also found Eleanor far from feeling well.

In one of those odd wrinkles of pregnancy, Eleanor had decided to come down with *afternoon* sickness. It hadn't taken long for Tracy to realize that it would be a good idea for her to go find herself a room and come back to Eleanor's tomorrow.

Purett's Inn was apparently tucked away at the east end of noplace-in-particular, although in actual distance it probably wasn't more than two or three miles away from Eleanor's front door. Maybe even less as the crow flew.

Provided the crow knew exactly where it was going, which Tracy didn't.

Finally she turned onto a quiet road—left, as she'd been directed—and found herself headed toward a batch of tall pine trees and beyond them a sprawling and rather ungainly-looking house that had to be the inn.

Lights were coming on in some of the rooms and there were also some larger floodlights outside illuminating the gravel driveway leading to a tiny parking area. Two cars were there and Tracy barely managed to squeeze hers up next to the classy dark blue Lexus that took up a space and a half all by itself.

She eased from the driver's seat, being careful not to tap her door into the gleaming finish of the other car. It was ticking over, the soft sound of a hot engine as it cools down and relaxes after a hard run. Apparently somebody else had also just arrived at the inn.

Pure Sin

Grabbing her luggage from her trunk, Tracy crunched her way to the front steps and stopped for a moment, taking her first good look at the property.

It was a rambling Victorian most probably, with paint that definitely needed refreshing. There were places where the gingerbread decorative trims had fallen away, while others were still in place. It certainly had potential—the bones of a lovely house were still visible in spite of the ravages of time and neglect.

She glanced at the old weathered sign propped up on the wraparound porch next to the front door. Some letters were missing—a couple of *t*'s and an apostrophe along with an *n*— and a shiver crossed her spine as she blinked at what was left.

"P-U-R-E S I-N."

The words were unmistakable, although Tracy knew very well what had been there originally. Her lips curved into a smile. It was delightfully whimsical and if she'd been asked then and there, she'd have told the owner not to touch it but to use it in an ad campaign.

"Spend the night—explore *Pure Sin*." Tag lines chased themselves through her brain and an entire marketing strategy exploded behind her eyes.

She chuckled and shook her head. It was definitely time to relax and leave that stuff behind for a bit if she couldn't even look at a broken sign without getting the urge to sell it to the masses.

The evening darkened behind her as Tracy walked up the wooden steps, across the porch and into Purett's Inn. She rested her cases next to her on the faded carpet as she looked around—and straight into the familiar eyes of a man she recognized.

"Good *God*."

"Well, I'll be..." He stared at her, a look of surprise on his face that probably matched hers.

"What the hell..."

"I can't believe…"

"*George?*"

"*Tracy?*"

"No. Montague Neville the Third." A raspy British voice interrupted the broken conversation and both heads swiveled to the desk where an elderly man was looking patiently up at the two of them. "But you can call me Monty. I'm assuming from your less-than-intelligible conversation that you've met before, didn't expect to see each other and plan on checking in." He tugged at a large book next to him.

"If my assumptions are correct, then I'd much appreciate your doing the latter first, since my bladder isn't all it used to be and I would hate to spoil what's left of this lovely Axminster by piddling on it."

Tracy moved to the desk. "Sorry. Yes, we have met. This is a surprise, George. Talk about a small world…" She settled her bag on the counter and pulled out a credit card. "Are you staying here too?"

"That depends." He moved to stand next to her and looked at the elderly receptionist. "You have rooms?"

One white eyebrow rose sarcastically. "We are an *inn*, sir. The function of an inn is to provide rooms for guests. If we only provided food, we'd be a restaurant, now wouldn't we?"

Chastened, George nodded. "Er, I guess."

"Well, that's good." Tracy signed the register while the old man jotted down her credit card number. "I'm here visiting a friend in town for a few days. So if you can give me a single for…maybe four nights?" She stared at Monty. "You have that available?"

"I believe so, madam." He lifted his chin. "There is a nice room on the second floor front that is suitable for ladies…bathroom *en suite* of course…"

"Of course." Tracy nodded. For the Brits, bathrooms sometimes found themselves not exactly *in* the guest room but down the hall. *En suite* was reassuring. She wouldn't have to wander down drafty passages to pee.

"Do I get to be *en suite* too?" A chuckle from her shoulder attracted Tracy's attention and she turned to see George smiling across the desk.

"I believe that can be arranged, sir. Would you care to be close to the lady?"

George's eyes widened and Tracy shivered a little as she watched his gaze turn hot. "I'd like that very much, Monty. Very much indeed." He hadn't moved, but Tracy felt the warmth from his body cross the space between them. All of a sudden there was a new fragrance in the air that only the two of them could detect.

It spelled out something basic, some attraction of male and female that was older than time and newer than anything Tracy could remember experiencing.

"Yes, I'm sure you would." Monty's acerbic tones shattered the brief intimacy. "Well, if you could manage to extricate your thoughts from whatever lurid fantasy you're enjoying at this moment, sir...and possibly give me a credit card, I'd be happy to provide *you* with a room as well."

Tracy bit down on her lip to avoid laughing out loud. George's expression had shot from sensual to embarrassed in less than a second. Monty seemed to be a law unto himself when it came to guests and Tracy wondered if any got scared away.

For her, Monty was a delight—like something out of a fancy British television show. She smiled as he passed her a key. A real, honest-to-God key with a tag attached displaying her room number.

"Cute." She glanced at it. "Two-B. Up the stairs and..."

"Turn right, madam." Monty passed over another key to George. "You will *also* turn right, sir. Your room is farther down. Two-D. And since you're going upstairs, you can flex those appealingly masculine muscles of yours by carrying the lady's bags, can't you? That way you'll impress her and spare me another trip to the chiropractor."

* * * * *

George grabbed Tracy's bags and grunted as he lifted them. Why women had to carry everything *including* the kitchen sink with them when they went anywhere, he had no frickin' clue. But they did. Sure as shit, they *always* did.

"Want me to take that one?" Tracy's voice came from behind him. "It's got my laptop and stuff in it."

He shook his head and ignored the hernia that was probably about to rip his guts to shreds as he moved across the foyer to the staircase. "You're not here on vacation, huh?"

She wrinkled her nose. "Well, sort of yes and sort of no."

"Ah. Hoookay. Glad you cleared that up."

A smile crossed her face. Damn she was beautiful when she smiled like that. George continued to watch her expressions as they climbed the stairs side by side.

"I have an old college friend in the area. She's married now and expecting their first baby. She suggested I come out for a visit and take a look at this place while I was here." Tracy paused at the top of the stairs and let her gaze wander around. "It's a nice building. Good potential."

"You an architect?" George wondered about her critical assessment.

"No." She chuckled. "I run an Internet marketing and promotions agency. Apparently one of Eleanor's friends is thinking of investing in the inn. She wanted to know if I thought it was marketable. You know…could I run a campaign to attract new guests, that sort of thing."

George hefted the bags more comfortably and led her down the hallway. "So you're doing on-the-job research…"

"Yeah. Sort of. I stay here while I visit Eleanor and get a good inside look at the inn at the same time."

"Handy arrangement." He paused in front of door number two-B. "This is you I think."

She turned and fiddled with her key in the lock. The door opened inward and she nodded. "Yep." She took the bags from him while propping the door open with one foot. "Thanks. I appreciate the help."

"Wait up a second…" *Jesus.* She was gonna shut the door on him. George was soooo not about to let that happen. "You hungry?"

"What?" She blinked at him.

"Hungry. You know. That odd feeling that makes your stomach gurgle at embarrassing moments and tells you that you'd better eat something soon?"

Tracy stared like it was some sort of comment she'd never heard before. "Huh?"

George sighed. "Look, *I'm* hungry. It's that time of day when most folks think about food. I'm thinking about food, so the odds are pretty good you're gonna be thinking about food too. If not right at this moment, then soon. So…" He paused, unsure of himself but determined. She could only say no. And maybe whack him stupid with her laptop.

What the hell. He'd already been accused of being stupid. He had nothing to lose. "Would you like to have dinner? With me?"

She swallowed. "Uh—sure. That would be—nice."

For once she seemed a little uncertain, not quite so much the professional woman-in-control of herself. It was almost like she hadn't expected to be asked out and didn't quite know what to do about it.

George was delighted. "Cool. I need to shower and unpack and I'm guessing you do too. So how about I pick you up in an hour?"

She raised an eyebrow. "Pick me up?"

He rolled his eyes. "Okay. Knock on your door." Women were so frickin' *literal* at times. "I'd like to go back into town—there's a real nice place there with a small deli restaurant next door where we can have a few drinks maybe afterward?"

Tracy tilted her head to one side and narrowed her eyes. "Would that be The Mating Place, by any chance? Right next door to The Eating Place?"

"Yeah. I think that's what it was called. The bar's run by a cool guy named Justin? A buddy of mine works for him and I came out to talk with him." He snapped his fingers. "Hey...you were there. Remember that huge picture at the art gallery where we met? The one with the woman...er..." He felt the heat rush to his cheeks. *Now you've dug yourself a nice hole, dickhead.*

Her cheeks were coloring up as well. "I remember the one. Vividly." She laughed.

"Well it's Marcus, the photographer, who I came to see. Turns out he works for Justin at the bar when he's not taking erotic photos. I want that picture. It sort of stayed in the back of my mind, you know?"

"Yeah." Tracy nodded. "It really was quite something. I wouldn't mind meeting this Marcus guy. He's one hell of a photographer." She stepped backward. "But I really should go unpack."

George straightened. "Yeah, me too. So I'll see you in about an hour then?"

She smiled. "Sure. I'm looking forward to it. But don't expect any city flash. I'm definitely doing comfortable jeans tonight."

"Sounds good to me. See you soon." George watched her door close and heard the key turn in the lock. Then he sauntered down the hallway to the next door and went into his own room.

He felt—energized. Charged up and ready to go party. He had a date—a *date* for God's sake—with Tracy. A dinner date that could lead to any number of things, visions of which ran erotically through his head as he absently unpacked and settled himself into the old-fashioned bedroom.

The bed was a bit hard and the uneven surface of the quilt hinted at a possibly lumpy mattress. *Hmmm.* He looked around.

"Where the hell is the TV remote? They usually glue them to the table. I need to check the news. Why am I talking to myself?" George stopped in his tracks, looked around and sighed. "Shit, there isn't even a TV in here."

There was one very large upholstered chair next to the well-worn bureau. A wing chair, possibly a reclining one. His mind wandered momentarily.

An image of Tracy, naked and bent over the padded arm, flashed before his eyes. He'd be thrusting into her from behind, his hands grabbing her hips as her dark hair swung freely and she sobbed out little moans of delight. He wondered if she was a noisy lover or a quiet one.

If she would scream when she came or just melt in breathless silence.

Heat flooded his body, pooling low in his groin and making him dizzy for a second or two. *Boinggg*…something about this woman had gotten to him. Maybe it was those doe-brown eyes of hers, lighting with humor when she laughed. Or perhaps it was that shape—curved in all the right places for a man to hold. She was no slender supermodel, but a vital and warm armful of flesh and pleasure.

George surprised himself with the force of his sudden need for her. Tina was a distant memory—fading very rapidly into the mists of his past. But he hadn't expected to find another woman quite so interesting quite so soon. He certainly wasn't looking for one.

But he *was* looking forward to dinner with her. He was hungry and he hoped she might be dessert. A warm and silky crème brulée that would be sweet on his tongue and soft around the rest of him.

He sighed. If he didn't get his ass in gear and change he'd never find out what kind of dessert Tracy was and in addition his own goose would get itself well and truly cooked.

A loud grumble from beneath his belt buckle made him wonder if his hard-on was growling. It was his stomach instead. George hurried to unpack and hit the shower, realizing as he did so that he was damn near as nervous as he could remember being in a long time.

He wondered if Tracy was nervous too.

Chapter Four

ಐ

Dinner had been fun.

Tracy and George were tucked away at a table in a shadowed corner of The Mating Place enjoying after-dinner drinks and listening to a couple of locals who were doing their best country music star impressions—and actually doing it very well.

Tracy leaned back and grinned. "This is nice."

George finished his beer and waved at the waitress. "Yeah, it is." He flicked his fingers over their glasses as the busy woman nodded at him. "And I hate country music and I'm still having fun."

"Oh lord. Another scotch?" Tracy giggled. "You're trying to get me drunk, aren't you?"

"But of course. It's my duty as a male." He saluted and laughed. "How am I doing?"

"Pretty damn good."

Tracy was surprised at herself. That wasn't the usual sort of comment she made. In fact, she was feeling quite unlike herself at this particular moment. Exactly who she *was* feeling like, she wasn't quite sure, but it certainly wasn't the cautiously buttoned-up woman who'd arrived at the Inn earlier in the day.

Nope, this woman was—looser. More relaxed. And, if she dared to admit it, more turned on. Something about George was stimulating in a delightfully sexual way. His smile caressed her and sent tiny shivers of arousal into places that had been asleep for quite some time. The expression in his eyes was warm and could turn hot in a microsecond.

Tracy liked that. She liked knowing he liked what he saw when he looked at her. She preened, letting her shirt fall open now and again to show off her cleavage. She had paid a lot for the bra supporting it after all. Might as well get her money's worth out of it.

And she was definitely feeling no pain. The smooth scotch she'd been enjoying was dulling any number of routine sensations while it cranked up her response to George. God bless liquor. She'd have been quite nervous without it, but as things stood—or sort of *leaned* a little—she was relaxed, aware of George on a purely feminine level and having a really, really nice time.

It seemed to Tracy as if something was building between them—something very fundamental. An awareness of each other, a silent mutual acceptance that they were both attracted to each other and considering the possibilities such an attraction presented.

Tracy couldn't help but notice George's gaze as it wandered over her body at irregular intervals. A little pulse thudded in his neck just above his collar and he would absently lick his lips.

In her turn, she watched his hands as they curved around his glass or lay still on the table. Large hands, capable hands, with fingers that tapered nicely. Hands and fingers that would probably feel most excellent around her breasts.

Okay, so scotch tended to bring out the hornies. *So sue me.* It wasn't against the law to have fantasies about one's date, especially when his name was George Cluny. A girl could dream.

But as the evening wore on, Tracy found she wasn't dreaming about any movie star at all—she was having increasingly hot fantasies about her own personal Cluny. He was, to put it plainly, turning her on. *Big* time.

They kept the conversation light and flirtatious, as if each of them realized where the potential for this night might be headed, but neither wanted to jeopardize it. Not right at this moment.

George reached over and brushed her cheek near her lips. "Got a bit of hair stuck there."

She leaned in to his hand, resting against his palm for a second longer than necessary. "Thanks."

He glanced around the bar. "Dance with me?"

Tracy blinked. The dance floor was, to be polite, small. The music—which had gone from live amateur country to recorded professional romantic—was alluring. The idea of snuggling in George's arms in front of the small number of patrons was even more appealing. "Okay."

It seemed natural to tuck her hand in his as he led her to a spot on the edge of the floor. Even more natural to turn and nestle into his chest as he pulled her hand between them and folded his around it, holding it close to his heart.

She sighed as his other hand splayed across the base of her spine and pulled her against him.

They fit. The planes and dips in his body seemed designed to match the curves and valleys of hers. Her head drifted to his shoulder and found the place where her cheek could rest comfortably, her nose millimeters from his neck.

He smelled good, she thought contentedly. Just like a real man should. Kind of outdoorsy and clean with a dash of musk and a hint of aftershave. It was a good smell, the kind you couldn't bottle or spray on. The kind that slipped into a woman's nostrils and made her think of delightfully wicked things.

She sighed and his arms tightened in response. "Tired?" George's breath stirred the hair around her ear and made her shiver.

"Not really. Just having a very nice time." She cuddled closer. "You're a good dancer."

This time his lips definitely brushed her head. "I'm glad. So are you. Feels good holding you like this."

Tracy smiled and shifted her position a little, closer to his skin. She wanted nothing more than to stick out her tongue and taste him. It was primeval, this need she had, drowning out the music and the people—just an overwhelming urge to get the essence of him onto her taste buds. To see if that matched her needs as well as his scent. To see if they were compatible in more ways than she'd yet discovered.

Drifting idly on her erotic fantasies, Tracy let herself go.

It was an unusually arousing sensation too, this feeling of contentment and awareness in a man's embrace. For once, there was no need for protective walls, socially appropriate chit-chat, or the withdrawal that had so often marked her interactions with her dates.

She was comfortable, happy, turned on and—as she'd just pointed out—having a *really* nice time. At some point in the future she'd probably be surprised by all of the above, but right now she was just enjoying the hell out of it.

And also enjoying the brush of George's very masculine body against hers as they moved slowly to the music. At least Tracy *assumed* they were moving to the music. She'd stopped hearing it right around the time he'd put his arms around her. Perhaps he should come with a warning label—*dancing with George may cause temporary deafness. Other side effects may include heightened sexual arousal and an increased urge to perform unusually erotic activities.*

This man was unique. Her reaction to him was unique. He'd bypassed the normal route to her interest and gone straight in under her radar to land front and center of her desires.

Tracy realized that her body was sending her messages that exactly coincided with the ones in her brain. Her panties were damp, her nipples were extremely sensitive where they were pressed into George's chest and his breath on her exposed skin was enough to make her shudder—and not from the cold.

She *wanted* him.

This stranger—well, *almost* stranger—this man who'd simply bought her dinner and laughed with her. Who'd danced with her, made her forget so many of her own rules and above all made her feel—*real*.

She wanted him. Wanted to get naked with him and have wild monkey sex. *Yearned* actually, rather than *wanted*. That was too mild a word for the emotions that were beginning to burn deep inside her.

And never, in her entire life, had she experienced what could be termed *wild monkey sex*.

She swallowed down a lump of what had to be lust, pure and simple. And apparently he heard her.

"Tracy…"

She turned her head on his shoulder to see him smile a little and then glance at her mouth. "I gotta do this…" He brushed his lips over hers, lightly, briefly, not half long enough for her tastes.

Even though it was the tiniest of kisses, she still moaned.

"Let's get out of here…" His arms banded her tightly for a second or two, steel muscles holding her clamped against him.

"Okay." She was *not* about to argue. Not when she'd just realized that there was a wonderfully hard bulge distorting the front of his jeans. She *wanted* that bulge. That was *her* bulge. She was solely responsible for that bulge and she fully intended to be solely responsible for making it go away.

Now she knew who she was feeling like. Somebody who'd been buried inside for too long. Somebody who'd simmered silently and patiently through the many didn't-quite-make-it relationships.

Tracy-the-wanton-slut was on the loose.

And grinning like an idiot.

* * * * *

George drove too fast, but what the hell. He had a horny wonderful woman next to him and time was wasting.

He toyed with the idea of pulling over for some hot in-the-front-seat sex. Then he dismissed the idea, since he wasn't nineteen anymore and he might break something important. Like the shift lever on his car, or a couple of vertebrae. His insurance probably wouldn't cover either of 'em.

Operating mostly on instinct, he got them back to the inn without incident—a miracle since the scent of Tracy's perfume lingered on his clothes and her body heat radiated from the seat next to him. She was a major distraction, a walking invitation to sex and he wondered if that lump in his throat might just be his balls.

He sort of wished she'd jump him, or strip off her panties and play with herself or do something vaguely porn-movie-like, just to extend the excitement of the moment. Not that his *excitement* needed any further extending, since it was pretty much swollen as far as his jeans would allow right now.

Thank God—the inn. George sprayed gravel from his rear wheels as he took the turn into the parking lot and then stomped on the brake in surprise.

The lot was damn near full. "That's odd."

Tracy was looking around as well. "Yeah. Where did all these cars come from?" She peered through the windshield. "I don't see that many lights in the house. I wonder what's up?"

George finally found a spot and tucked the Lexus in between a rather elegant British sedan and another low-slung sports car of indefinable parentage. "Maybe it's the European sports-car owners convention or something." He got out and came around to help Tracy negotiate the ruts in the gravel. "Watch your step."

She stumbled a little as her sneaker hit a pile of stones but caught his hand and stayed upright. "Whoops. Thanks."

Slipping naturally under his arm, she held his waist with her free hand and together they crunched toward the front door.

"This many cars—gotta be fifty or so people." George blinked at the lot. "Oh maybe it's a party or a reception…"

The throaty roar of a motorcycle interrupted him and they both turned to see a very large and gleaming machine snuggle into a parking space that seemed to be awaiting that very beast. The riders dismounted and opened up various containers, stowing helmets and jackets.

"Uh, George?" Tracy squeezed his waist and whispered.

He whispered back. "I see it."

What he saw was a woman, tall and shapely, her body now revealed as she peeled off her bike gear. She wore a very tight leather corset, leather boots and not much else. With her was a shorter man, also in leather, with long graying hair pulled back into a ponytail. His clothes consisted of a leather vest over a bare chest, black shiny pants and heavy bike boots.

And a leash.

The end of which he was attaching to a spiked black leather collar his date wore around her neck.

Nodding, he stepped back, spun on his heel and tugged. His date followed—not having many other options since she was now at the end of the leash he held firmly. They disappeared through a small gate and around the side of the inn, leaving George and Tracy staring after them open-mouthed.

"Uhhh…"

"I'll be damned…"

"There's something you don't see too often." Tracy gulped. "Er, George?"

She waved her hand in front of his face, trying to get his attention. He was still staring at the leather-clad brunette. "What?"

"Wanna go see what's happening?"

He blinked and focused down on Tracy's face as she stared at him. There was a distinctly wicked gleam in her eyes. "You mean like go and spy on people who probably prefer a lot of privacy?"

"Yep."

George felt a grin curve his lips. "Oh hell yes."

Carefully and quietly they followed the path the other two had taken, trying to keep their footsteps as silent as possible. It wasn't easy given the gravel underfoot and the fact that Tracy had a tendency to hum every now and again.

"Sssh. You're humming."

"Am not."

"Yes you are. Sounds like...um...some kids' cartoon theme? Those little blue fuzzy dudes?"

"Nope. Not me."

George sighed and gave up. *No point in arguing with a woman who's got several scotches under her belt.* He wondered if he'd ever remember the name of those blue critters.

As they rounded the corner of the house, lights and noise greeted them, the lights shining from two or three uncovered windows and the noise muffled by the shrubbery that surrounded a huge barn. George wasn't surprised he hadn't seen it before—he hadn't exactly mapped out the territory and it was very well concealed by lots of trees and bushes.

But given the activity obviously going on inside, *somebody* knew where it was. Quite a few somebodies.

"Aha." Tracy slipped from his arm and tiptoed toward one side of the old building. "This is where they're hanging out. Come on. Let's go take a look."

George shrugged. What could it hurt? Just a quick glance in through the window and then he planned on whipping Tracy out of the shrubs and into bed. And whipping something else out as well.

At that inopportune moment, a brainwave hit him. He snapped his fingers. "The *Smurfs*."

There was a silence for a moment or two as Tracy peeked around a half-closed shutter.

Then she chuckled. "Oh I don't think so, George. No, I don't think so *at all*."

Chapter Five

"Shit. I can't see properly..." Tracy frowned as she stumbled a little after standing on tiptoe to peek through into the barn.

"Okay—here, try this." George noticed an old wooden crate a little way away and tugged it over, steadying it beneath the window. "Will this work?"

Tentatively she put her hand on George's shoulder and stepped up onto the wood, which, thankfully, held her weight. "Oh my God. Yeah. Now I can see...holy *shit*."

"What, Tracy? Whaddya see?" George fidgeted beneath her grasp.

"Shhh."

The light from inside the big space wasn't very bright so Tracy had to blink and squint to focus. But it only took a few moments for her eyesight to adjust.

And to see—within a few feet of the window—a naked man.

He was blindfolded and tied by his wrists and ankles to some sort of wooden cross-like thing. And there were two women, one on either side, dressed similarly in black leather vests and fishnet tights. And apparently nothing else.

Tracy sucked in a breath as one woman reached over to a small table, grabbed something and then clipped it onto the man's nipple. He shuddered, the light catching a sharp object and the chain that dangled from it. He shuddered again as she attached the end to his other nipple.

And jerked on the chain.

Pure Sin

He cried out, a yell of pain, tempered with a groan. His cock was hard and grew even harder as the woman played with the nipple chain, licking around the clamps every now and again between tugs.

The second woman took his cock in her fist and stroked him, gently moving her grasp up and down in a soothing yet arousing caress that made his thighs tremble.

Tracy watched his muscles as they twitched and shivered all over his body. His arms and legs strained against their bonds and his hips thrust forward, moving his cock in a frantic effort to hasten the second woman's strokes.

As if this was some sort of sign, the two women slipped off their vests, leaving themselves naked all but for the skimpy fishnet stockings. They continued their assault, but the second woman now knelt between the man's legs and took his cock into her mouth instead of her hands.

Tracy watched her head move as she sucked him and then gasped as the other woman passed her friend another set of clamps—and they were applied to the man's balls.

"What can you see?" George was fidgeting a lot. "What the hell's going on, Tracy?"

"Uhh…you ever had your balls clamped?"

There was a sound that Tracy correctly interpreted as George sort of crossing his legs protectively while standing up. "No."

"Okay. Then you probably won't want to see this."

"You're kidding, right?"

"Shh."

As she re-focused on the scene in front of her, the man surrendered to his two dominatrixes and let go, coming in spurts over whichever woman could get in front of him and claim his come. They seemed to take turns, stroking, pulling, milking his cock of every single drop and rubbing it over each other, lingering at breast and nipple. Others had gathered to watch and Tracy noticed several onlookers reaching in to be part of the fun.

She took a deep breath as the man was untied and led limply away. The wooden structure remained empty.

It seemed as good a time as any to let George take a look.

"So it seems like this little inn has a secret life going for it." She turned and carefully stepped down from the crate.

"Yeah?" George was craning his neck.

"Oh yeah." Tracy swallowed. She'd been turned on by what she saw, no doubt about it. When combined with the effect George was having on her, along with the scotch, Tracy was now one *very* horny lady.

A curious one too. Not the wisest combination at any time. "Yeah…we've managed to find ourselves a genuine BDSM club, George."

"No shit. Really?"

"Take a look for yourself."

She waved him up onto the crate, closing her eyes and just breathing for a moment or two. George's scent sneaked into her nostrils—warm, male and musky—accompanied by lurid images of the two of them together getting kinky.

His hip brushed her arm as he clambered up and Tracy daringly reached out for his thigh under the pretext of steadying both of them.

"Uhhh…" George held quite still. "You okay?"

"Mmmm." She leaned against him, enjoying the hardness of his hips and letting her hand move up a little, stopping just short of his crotch.

"No clamps in your bag or anything?"

"They're in my other purse."

"Okay. Just checking." George sounded relieved as he turned back to the window.

Tracy opened her eyes again and glanced up at him. He had one hand leaning on the wall beside the window as he peered through the dirty glass. She waited. She pretty much knew what his next words were going to be.

"*Holy fucking shit.*"

* * * * *

George had, up until this moment, considered himself a pretty well-educated guy when it came to sex. He'd seen and done most things, survived college, had affairs and made it through his relationship with Tina to emerge with a whole skin. He knew which end was up and how to go down.

He'd seen and heard enough about BDSM to get a firm idea of what-all was involved and the erotic art he'd seen in the gallery a while ago confirmed much of what he'd imagined.

This, however, was something *else* again.

George felt his jaw drop as he peered in to what could easily have modeled for some sort of Dante's Inferno as imagined by a perverted biker on drugs. For a second or two, he wondered if he'd lost his ability to see colors, since everything seemed to be black leather or white skin. He blinked and leaned closer to the window.

Although a twenty-first-century man on the surface, George immediately reverted to caveman drooling at the amazing array of naked female breasts.

All shapes and sizes, they swung freely, bobbed, bounced and generally enjoyed themselves without the benefit of covering or support. Some were thinly veiled by fishnet garments, others sported jewelry dangling from, or pinching, nipples that were, overall, pretty hard. Perhaps it was cold inside or perhaps the owners of said nipples were turned on.

The latter was most likely, all things considered. Once his eyeballs adjusted, George also noticed an unusual number of naked pussies as well. Not *everybody* was nude though — it seemed to be an individual decision.

And as a well-hung, erect man strolled past, he realized it was *not* a decision restricted to women either. A sharp movement from one side drew his attention and he gasped at the sight of a totally naked blonde being lowered to a table and secured by wrist and ankle. Her legs were splayed wide and George had a view that rivaled any her gynecologist probably got at her last physical exam.

"What's going on?" A voice hissed at him from someplace around his fly. He'd almost forgotten Tracy, but her question reminded him that she was still holding his leg. Pretty tightly too.

"Um...well, there's this naked blonde..."

A gusty sigh greeted his words. "Figures." The hands gripping his leg tightened a little bit. "Pretty wild stuff, huh?"

A tingly feeling rippled through his cock as Tracy's fingers moved. "Yeah. Pretty wild."

Between the woman next to him and the women inside the barn, George's furnace was getting a damn good stoking. Not that it needed it, but all the same...

More fuel got heaped on his fire as a man stepped between the naked blonde's legs and settled himself at eye level to her pussy. At the same time, another man moved next to her body and placed a coil of what looked like laundry line on her abdomen, complete with little wooden clothespins.

George blinked. "Whaddya know?"

"What?"

"If she was wearing anything I'd say they were gonna do a load of clothes in the washer..." He stared. "Oh shit."

"What?" Tracy repeated her question, her palms burning his skin through his jeans.

"There's this guy...he's sitting in front of her...her...well, he's...*God.*"

"Which one? The God of Leather? The God of BDSM? Slappy, the minor deity in charge of spanking?"

"No, he's *eating* her out. Honest. Right there in front of everybody." George shivered as he watched the skilled tongue of the seated man begin arousing the blonde with long, slow licks of her pussy.

There was silence for a moment as George watched the erotic display. "Now the other man—the one with the clothesline—he's...oucheeeeee!"

Tracy's hand was now millimeters from his cock. "What, George? Tell me..."

George gulped. "He's clipping those peg things to her ti—uhhhh—her breasts. Her nipples to be exact. And down to her bellybutton..."

"It's exciting you, isn't it?" Fingers brushed the hardness of his cock through the fabric. "Unless your car keys are part of some expanding universe..."

George grinned, although somewhat painfully. "Those aren't my car keys, dear."

She chuckled. "No kidding." Blatant now, her hand found his erection and explored it. "That's a helluva hard-on, mister."

He snorted, torn between embarrassment and pride. "Hell, this is one stimulating show. Sort of like watching porn, only no close-ups and money shots."

At that moment the group around the blonde moved. The guy with the pegs ripped them off in one swift pull on the rope connecting them at the very moment the guy between her legs thrust his face into her pussy and ground his mouth into her clit.

She screamed and came in shuddering tremors of restrained limbs, her mouth open on an orgasmic shriek. Two other men stepped from the shadows and stroked themselves frantically, erupting within seconds onto her body and spattering the red marks on her breasts and abdomen with their come.

"Okay. This *has* money shots." George almost choked on the words. "Shit. I wonder what it's like…"

"What *what's* like?"

"Having a woman do *anything*." He stared as a man led a woman around by a leash. She was naked and her eyes were downcast as she followed. Leashes were clearly in vogue this year.

"You mean *dominating* her?" Fingernails dug into his leg and George pulled his attention back from the scene inside the barn to the woman outside the barn. The one who seemed fascinated with his cock.

"Yes." It was an honest response. He did wonder what it would be like.

"Why don't you try it and find out?"

The words stunned George and he looked down into Tracy's upturned face, trying to sense her mood. Then he remembered. He'd seen her transfixed like this before when she stared at the photo in the gallery. The flicker of light from the window set the flakes of color in her eyes ablaze with fire.

"What would you like, George? Right this minute? If you were my Master, what would you desire?"

"Tricky question." He forced his gaze away from her mouth and back into the barn, only to see a man tugging a bound and naked woman to her knees and bending her over a low stool. She had some kind of contraption buckled around her head and in her mouth, holding her jaws apart in an "O".

As the man dropped his pants, George realized the purpose of this device. And his cock leapt to attention.

"Mmm. Good idea." Tracy was staring at his fly.

George cleared his throat. "Okay." He could do this. Between the sex inside and the sexy woman outside, he could definitely do this. "I want a blowjob." She didn't run screaming. That was good.

"*Now.*"

He tried to sound as forceful as a man could when telling a woman to blow him. George wasn't exactly used to *telling* a woman to do it either. It was more a whimpering begging sort of request, so he had to struggle to get the words out in a dominating tone.

Gentle fingers found his zipper and slid it down. He shivered as the night air found hot, hard flesh inside his briefs. "Tracy…"

"Ssshhh. You watch the show. I have a task to perform…for my Master."

He wasn't totally sure where this was going until Tracy freed him and quickly pulled his body close. Warmth encased George's cock as it slid between her lips.

Her hands clamped onto his ass and she began moving, sliding her tongue over him, slicking him with her saliva and sucking him with strong tugs of her tongue.

George glanced through the window and saw the man finding a comfortable stance as he thrust himself through the gag into *his* woman's mouth. Absently, his hips thrust in a matching rhythm. For those moments he shared an experience with a stranger—an erotic and masterful possession of a woman's mouth.

Tracy moaned deep in her throat as George began to fuck her mouth as if it were her pussy. He panted and just remaining in control was a strain on his senses. His passion had been aroused by the exposure to sights he'd barely even imagined, let alone watched happen between real people.

Now Tracy was there, submitting to his request, offering to please him. It gave him an incredibly erotic feeling of empowerment that overwhelmed him with delight. George explored the completely new and intoxicating sensation that this moment was just for *him*.

He began to lose his balance as his knees weakened. Tracy sucked George in and squeezed his ass hard. Distracted, torn between Tracy and the couple inside, George struggled to hold back, lost in some sort of sexual fog created by excessive oral pleasure and accompanied by wonderful sucking sounds.

His muscles tensed and as the man inside the barn threw his head back and snarled out his orgasm, George felt his own beginning. His fingers curled into a fist and unconsciously he pounded it on the wall of the barn.

The same wall that separated them from the people inside had become his sounding board and now everyone *inside* knew someone was *outside*.

Tracy yanked her head from his cock at the very last moment, bringing a second or two of clarity to his trembling brain. "Shit, George…cut that out for Chrissake…"

"Whoops!" Realizing what he'd done, George stumbled down off the crate and grabbed Tracy's arm. "C'mon. Let's get out of here." They hurried back along the path to the inn.

In his haste, George had forgotten something, however. It was recalled to his mind with a vengeance when he tried to zip up his fly. *A man should always tuck his cock back inside before attempting to rezip.* His whimper of exquisite agony didn't seem to get a reaction from Tracy, but she was having her own troubles running over the uneven path in her scotch-enhanced state.

George felt a grin curve his mouth as they stumbled toward the relative safety of the inn. Perhaps this whole dominance thing needed some further exploration. And perhaps Tracy would be the one exploring it with him.

As his submissive.

Just the thought was enough to send his cock into overload once more and he rushed Tracy inside, through the lobby and up the stairs like he was in the last seconds of an Olympic sprinting event.

He *wanted* her. Any way he could get her. Dominant—submissive—black leather or blue denim. It didn't matter. The only thing that mattered right now was fucking Tracy.

Chapter Six

The cold wooden wall of her room hurt Tracy's back as George's body ground against hers with lustful pressure. Her breath hitched in her throat, caught up in the flood of desire billowing inside her.

George's mouth bruised her lips with wet and hard kisses. There wasn't going to be a handshake or a cordial good night here. This was going to be bareback fucking at its best and most animalistic.

Or at least she hoped so.

Tracy slid her tongue into George's mouth, letting heat radiate from their passion as he sucked it in. She wanted him. No—more than that—she *needed* him and the scorching heat between her thighs reinforced that need. She'd experienced sexual tension before, but this was different. This had a color and a flavor all its own—a unique desire that Tracy struggled to comprehend.

She wanted to surrender. To give George anything and everything he wanted. To hand over this entire experience to him. To be the lead violinist in the orchestra of sexual pleasure he was conducting. It was a strange, almost frighteningly intense, desire and one that scared her a little.

And it looked like George had his own needs.

He reached up and grabbed a handful of Tracy's blouse, pausing at the sound of tearing fabric.

Tracy frowned. "Hey, be careful. I..." The words tapered off as she stared at him, looking at the heavy-lidded eyes, the heat in his gaze and the flush of color flooding his cheeks. "Go ahead, George. Do it. *Rip it.* I don't care. Do what you want. Take what you want..."

Pure Sin

He gave a little nod then licked his lips, tore the fabric and stared at the skin of her neck and shoulder. His mouth brushed against it while Tracy rested her hands on the back of his head.

George traced the strap of her bra with his lips then glided his hand along her waist and cupped her breast through the remnants of her blouse. The fullness swelled in the bra cup, almost spilling free from the confinement.

Tracy's hands instinctively pulled his head, urging it downward to where her nipples ached for attention. A fire in her was blazing but George remained solidly unmoving. She risked a glance at him.

He spoke. "*Wait.*"

It was one word, but it told Tracy so much more. It told her *he* was in control and that knowledge was enough to send the tension between them skyrocketing through the roof.

She trembled, obediently waiting for his next command. She knew now she had met a man whose curiosity matched her own. Whose needs might prove equal or even greater than hers.

A man on the edge—as she was—of finding a new approach to sex.

"What do you want?" She risked the whisper, unsure of where to move, what to do, what to say. This was all virgin territory for Tracy and she was confused.

"Unzip your jeans and open your legs to me."

There was no hesitation now in George's voice. He *knew*.

He knew what she was offering and he was taking it.

Tracy's pussy wept with excitement as she released his head and obeyed his orders. She opened her pants, parting the fabric around her silk underwear and letting it hang loosely on her hips.

Slowly, George went down on one knee in front of her then reached his hands around the backs of her legs, brushing the tense muscles. He found the mounds of her buttocks, grabbed them—and squeezed. She sighed out a soft laugh of pleasure as he kneaded her, each touch an arousal by itself.

"Move your panties. I want to see you." His gaze was on her pussy, concealed by its flimsy covering of silk.

Sucking in a breath, Tracy again obeyed, a lick of heat searing through her as she reached down and pulled the delicate material aside. The cool air brushed hot folds of swollen flesh and she felt heat flooding her face as George did nothing but stare at her.

Tracy ached. She wanted to shove her pussy into his face, scream at him to devour her, force his head in between her thighs.

But she did none of those things. Because he had not given her permission and she just *knew* she wasn't supposed to ask.

A quick, sharp tug and what was left of her blouse fell away. Her bra followed, victim to George's need to see her naked before him. Eagerly he ripped her clothes off her, his very eagerness a sensual arousal all by itself.

It was amazing to know a man wanted her *this* much.

And finally he took what he wanted. A handful of breast, cupped firmly in a strong palm. The nipple thumbed with fervor, quick sharp flicks of a nail sending electric shocks through Tracy's body to her cunt.

He suckled her, his mouth pulling hard on the tender nub even as his other hand sought the moisture of her pussy. He explored, matching moves with mouth and hands, sometimes gentle, sometimes not.

He was thorough, exploring where he wanted to explore, amazing Tracy with the way his mouth found the exact spots that yearned for his touch. She didn't need to guide him, she barely even touched him. It was more a case of submitting to his caresses with a willingness to surrender that astounded her.

Finally he returned to kneel in front of her and with a quick rough move her jeans and panties were pulled to her ankles and then tossed aside completely. Naked now, she shivered—but not with cold.

Being like this—totally nude—while he was still dressed...well, it was a turn-on of major proportions. Tracy knew her thighs were wet and the throb of her pussy pounded loudly throughout her entire body.

Her breasts ached and involuntarily her hands moved a little, upward, yearning to take the heated weight from her shoulders. But—mindful of the new rules to this game—she paused as an idea took shape in her mind. "George. May I touch my breasts?"

It was a daring, whispered question, one that she suddenly realized would take them both onto a path leading into the mists of a new place, a dark and hotly passionate place that Tracy so wanted to explore.

"Yes." His voice was a harsh croak and his gaze burned as she lifted her hands to cradle her breasts.

With a groan of his own, George finally fulfilled Tracy's fantasies. He lifted her leg onto his shoulder and dove his face into her wet and swollen folds of flesh.

She cried out and shut her eyes tightly as George's mouth suckled her pussy. He put just enough pressure behind his tongue to make her crazy and when he found crevices between the slippery flesh, she shook with delight. She could feel the painful pleasure of her clit, aroused and sensitive to his every move, every breath.

He was giving her what she wanted. He was taking what she offered.

And George was in control.

Tracy surrendered, submitted and, for once in her life, let go.

* * * * *

George couldn't get enough. His mouth and tongue could only get so deep and the awkward position made him only more frustrated. He wanted to eat her pussy properly before they fucked into oblivion. His cock was straining in his pants. It too wanted Tracy, in the worst way.

He pulled back. A trickle of her juice fell from his lips.

He continued his stare at her swollen folds of flesh. "Damn you have a great pussy. I bet it feels like velvet inside." He was speaking his thoughts aloud.

Tracy only moaned. He hoped she was seeing the vision of him buried within her. It was time to move, to take this dance someplace George could manage more comfortably. Rapidly he swept her off her feet and tumbled her onto the bed, burrowing back between her naked thighs before she had chance to do more than gasp his name.

George knew he had control but there was something missing. He loved a woman talking while he licked the succulent juices from her cunt. Her voice telling him all the things she was feeling, along with what she liked—he needed to hear her.

He pulled his mouth free, letting her honey drip from his chin. "Tracy, you can talk. I want to hear your voice when I eat you and hear you scream when we fuck."

George lowered his mouth back between her legs. Tracy was writhing and letting him know she was beside herself with pleasure. He released some control to her but the only thing she could say was, "Oh God, that feels—*mmm*." Her words softly rolled into another moan.

George smiled because he knew he was on the right path. When he felt the firm bud in her pussy, he'd found heaven for both of them. He zeroed in on her clit, focused on bringing her to the brink of sanity before letting her go. Her squirms and whimpers signaled his tempo and the depth of his tongue.

Pure Sin

"Oh George—oh right—right—oh my God, I'm almost—" Her body felt tense and rigid. Tracy gasped for breath as she shuddered, shivering on the cusp of ecstasy.

George stopped and kissed her flinching stomach. "You can't come until I do, Tracy. You have to wait for me."

He knew there were only two ways Tracy could react to him. She could cross her legs and break his nose. Or she could try to stifle her growing need to come from his continued incredible teasing assault on the swollen tip of her engorged clit.

She would be torn and probably wondering if she could regain control. If she could hang on to herself and her body long enough to satisfy them both.

George was incredibly turned on by his new empowerment—his cock was so hard it hurt. He lifted his body away from Tracy's dripping pussy and tugged off his clothes, a frantic striptease that seemed to take hours longer than it should have. He wanted to take her like an animal. He wanted no-holds-barred *fucking*.

Looking down, he saw the gleam of wetness encompassing her folds of flesh. He panted and his ears rang with the hard pounding in his chest. He wanted her so badly. "I can't wait anymore. This is torture…keep playing with your breasts. I like watching you."

He dug his wallet from his back pocket and pulled out an older condom kept for special occasions and emergencies. From the way he wanted to thrust into Tracy's pussy with his cock, this was a real, honest-to-God emergency. He stood at the foot of the bed, staring at her body, ready, wet and waiting for him.

"Now open your pussy for me." George watched her short nails flash as she split the labia of her pussy apart.

Tracy lifted her hands away from her breasts free and laid them on either side of her mound, seeking the moisture and swollen flesh. For her, this was a small measure of payback. Even though George had taken control—with her full consent—she gained the pleasure of knowing she was helping him along, encouraging him, driving him to take that final plunge into her body.

She watched George's eyes widen. His cock strained skyward and fueled this inferno she felt burning inside her cunt. She saw him fumble with the condom and licked her lips at the sight of the drip of excitement beading the tip of his cock. Lord how she wanted him. How could she let him know? Words seemed so—*useless* at this point, even if she could have found anything to say. So she began to swirl her finger over her clit, legs shaking from her self-induced pleasure.

"Mmm, damn. I can't wait to fuck that tight little pussy." His voice was harsh and deep.

Tracy knew she was getting to George but also arousing herself. She wanted—no, *needed*—to feel his cock punishing her cunt so she could release this river of frustrating climaxes damned up inside her. Just the thought alone was enough to make her insert her finger, a tiny prelude to the oncoming feel of his cock.

George began to sweat, beads of moisture glittering on his forehead. Sure, she'd given him control but clearly trying to remain calm was hard. He almost looked as if he was fighting an urge to grab his cock and whack off. Tracy wondered how he felt having a nude woman splayed before him and opening her pussy to his gaze.

He stepped forward and reached down to grab each of her ankles. Pulling them up roughly, he let his cock press against her pussy. The pressure alone almost took Tracy over the edge. She tried to move her hips and angle that thick shaft where she so wanted it to be.

George turned his head to kiss the ankle he held firm in his grasp. He shifted and did the same thing to her other ankle. Then he pushed her legs apart and let the head of his cock enter Tracy's wet pussy. With a deep breath he fell forward, thrusting into her.

She arched her back, pushing against George's chest, meeting his body each time he pounded into her. Loud slaps began to echo in the room as their flesh collided, her mouth fell open and she gasped for air. The relentless toying with her pussy and the excitement had built to such a crescendo that it wasn't going to take much longer.

Tracy felt the heat radiating from George's body. "Oh fuck, your pussy is so fucking good. Shit, this is *incredible*." She saw his arms flex as he strained to keep his body weight from crashing onto her. His cock hammered deeply into her and the urge to erupt was growing with each plunge.

Tracy couldn't help her cry. "Make me come—George—you're making me *come*. Come with me, George. Fuck my pussy, fuck me, *fuck*…" She clenched her muscles around him, losing herself in the fire that burned now, consuming her.

"Oh fuck, keep that up. Oh my God, I can feel your pussy tightening around my cock." His voice cracked on the words.

"I'm going to come, George, come *on*, come with me."

Tracy began to shake and her toes curled as the wave of passion washed over her. She arched upward, driving her head back and exploded. Great racking shudders swamped her as she fell into a massive orgasm. Every muscle in her body was taut and trembling as she cried out harsh sounds of ecstasy. She was soaked with her own juices and still coming, still riding a wave of pleasure that shocked the crap out of her. She was afraid she was coming so hard she'd squirt out her juices.

George drove in one last time and as Tracy's spasms continued, he let go. Hot jets of seed shot deep into her cunt, sending more tremors coursing through her. George could barely hold his body up, even though his body still jerked and he still throbbed inside her.

Eventually, their bodies surrendered, easing down from the peak they'd shared, and they both lay for a few breathless moments in a tangled mess of sweaty limbs and flesh. Slowly George peeled himself off Tracy, pulling his cock from her and staggering to the bathroom.

Tracy heard a mumble and then the toilet flushed. She didn't move—she couldn't. Her body was too tired to do anything except lie there, dripping into the sheets. She felt like a waterlogged amoeba, all boneless and wet. "What did you say?"

With a thud he flopped onto the bed next to her. "I was thanking the condom factory for making these things extra durable. I swear to God they could make tires from 'em. Fuck, Tracy, that was—*incredible*."

"Yeah." She closed her eyes. "It sure was."

Much later George snuffled himself awake to a dark room and the scent of some real heavy sex. He breathed in, loving the fragrance of warm woman, wet pussy and a night of hot fucking. Seasoned with a dash of male sweat.

Tracy was snoring quietly beside him, sprawled half on his chest and half on the covers she'd swiped some time during their post-coital nap. He shifted a little, wondering if she would wake.

But she was dead to the world, limp and sound asleep.

George rested his head comfortably on the pillow and thought things over. This entire episode had been unexpected. All kidding aside, he really *had* made this trip only to visit his old buddy Marcus, not have hot sex with a really gorgeous babe. He wouldn't have changed a minute of it, but right at this moment he was sort of undecided about how to handle it.

The whole fetish thing in the barn—the way it had turned them both into horny little fuckers—shit. There was some stuff going on that George needed time to think about.

And he knew damn well that if Tracy woke up they'd be going at it again like rabbits within seconds flat. It had been *that* good between them. And yeah, he'd liked the moments when he'd been in total control. When Tracy had made it pretty damn clear she was surrendering to him.

A vision of her tied to the bed, naked, flashed through his head and straight down to his cock. He pushed it away. She was sleeping and it wouldn't be gentlemanly to wake her only to tie her up and fuck her all over again.

At least he didn't *think* it would be gentlemanly. His cock, of course, disagreed, signaling its opinion by hardening once more. Proud of his recuperative abilities, George smiled and mentally sent a message to his groin. "Good boy. Down. Stay."

The visions of her tied up were followed by ones of her tied to the bed face down, with her gorgeous ass all tipped up and ready for—what? His palm itched. Yeah. He wondered if a spanking or two would go over okay with her.

He kind of thought it would.

So how on earth could he possibly suggest to this woman he'd barely met, fucked to the point of exhaustion and then fallen asleep next to, that he'd rather like to slap her ass the next time they did it?

He wasn't a violent man and wouldn't hurt a fly. A mosquito, sure, but a fly? Not unless it got into his car and flew up his nose when he was driving—

George shook his head. This was getting a bit stupid and his mind was wandering. His cock shrank a little as a small headache began behind one ear. He really needed some time to put this stuff in order in his *own* mind before he talked to Tracy about it.

Silently, he crept from the bed, retrieved what he could of his clothes and slipped into his pants before leaving Tracy's room for his own.

He needed an aspirin or two, a shower, a clean pair of briefs and some quiet time to work out what had happened tonight. And where it would lead—tomorrow.

Chapter Seven

෨

Tracy wasn't quite sure what woke her.

Perhaps it was a car outside, or a slammed door—whatever it was, it worked. And the fact that she was alone became apparent immediately when she turned over and found herself reaching for empty space.

Fuck. She'd been walked out on. For a minute or so, she just shook—whether from rage or pain she wasn't quite sure.

It was out of character for her to have amazingly erotic sex with somebody she didn't know very well. It was totally out of character for her to scream when she came. Come to think of it, it really wasn't like her to come at all. Or at least very often. The few occasions she'd actually climaxed were more the sort of gentle rolling delight that poets probably wrote about using metaphors like "sunsets" and "cuddles".

She'd never hit high C like she'd done with George.

Never. *Ever.*

And now the bastard had left her high and dry. She pushed back the covers and slid her legs over the side of the bed with a groan. Okay, not dry exactly. More like sticky and rather stiff.

She sighed and headed for the bathroom, feeling a lot better once she'd dragged on a robe and tidied away the remains of their wild night. Force of habit drove her to her laptop, which she booted up. She doubted there was much going on she needed to know about, but checking her email was part of her life—as much a part as brushing her teeth or making coffee in the mornings.

Curling into the chair in front of the screen, Tracy gazed idly at the headings as she scrolled through her inbox. Nothing of interest—a few notes from business associates, a reply from the local Chamber of Commerce about the general area and the usual assortment of junk mail advertising fabulous mortgage rates, erectile dysfunction medications and ways to lose twenty pounds while she slept.

Sighing, she wrinkled her nose. She hadn't lost twenty pounds. She'd lost about a hundred and ninety pounds—of living, breathing, walking *man*.

The very last and most recent email snagged her eye. The sender was *NotthatGeorge* and it came from a well-known message host.

Tracy unbent her legs and leaned forward, clicking on the message to read it. Could it be from *her* George?

She sucked in a breath when she realized that it *was*. The first words gave him away...

"Hi Tracy. I hated to leave you..."

She bit back a tiny sound, a sob of relief perhaps at the realization he *hadn't* deserted her. Eager to learn more, she tugged her robe more securely around her shoulders and began to read.

I found your email address on that card you gave me at dinner. It seemed easier to write you, since I've got stuff going on in my head that's confusing me. And you're part of it.

First, I want to tell you how great you were—how great tonight was. Don't think I've ever had one quite like it. You are so damn hot, well, just thinking about you gets me hard. Yeah, even after the things we did. If I was there now, you wouldn't be reading your email, that's for sure."

Tracy shivered a little, but not from the cold. George was right. If he was there right now... She read on.

Anyway, now that you know I just needed to sort out my thoughts a bit, let me try to explain. It's kinda strange, you know? We don't know each other real well, but somehow tonight we connected in more ways than one. I guess getting to look in on those folks in the barn – well, I have to say it turned me on. I mean it REALLY turned me on. Like that rabbit that keeps going and going and going.

Now before you start thinking I'm a kinky pervert, I want you to know I'm not. Well, I may be a pervert, just not THAT kind. I've never been into any sort of bondage scene. Never played much with toys, other than my stuffed bear and the occasional vacuum attachments. I used to…well, never mind.

Thing is, Tracy, I think I'd sort of like to try some of that stuff. Not the hurting stuff – that's not my style. But being in control? Yeah, control…being in charge, the big cheese, calling the shots, I don't mean to get carried away but you affected me in a way I can't explain. In a good way.

Does this mean there's something wrong with me? Should I get therapy? Am I talking with the other brain? I don't know.

I also don't know if I could've said these things to you in person. I'm not really in control of very much in my life – not the things that matter. So this way, I can let you know what I'm thinking without worrying you're gonna give me one of those "go drop dead, you kinky freak" looks that women do so well. By the way, why can women give those looks that make a man feel about as tall as a cockroach and men can't?

So…um…there we are. I'm going to send this now. Don't know when you'll read it, but I feel better knowing that at some point you will.

Sincerely,

Not THAT George.

Tracy leaned back in her chair, mind awhirl.

She reread the email twice, trying to get her own thoughts sorted out into some kind of order. Was he asking her to explore this whole scene with him? Or was he just thinking aloud and emailing his confusion?

She didn't know and from the sound of things, he wasn't too sure either.

Closing her eyes, Tracy examined her own feelings. Yeah, she'd been turned on by that whole bondage thing as well. He'd said he wasn't in control of his life very much—she had the opposite problem.

Total control.

No chance to just sit back and hand over the reins to somebody else. And just thinking about doing that—in bed—with someone special...*Jesus*. Her pussy flooded as she considered the infinite possibilities.

What would it be like? To let a man really tell her what to do, when to do it and how? To be obedient to his every whim, knowing that she was pleasing herself just as much as she was pleasing him?

She'd sort of dabbled around the edges of that idea tonight—playing the submissive role for a little while, surrendering to George and asking his permission to touch herself.

What if she'd not had the choice? If he'd taken over completely, dominating her, bending her to his will? What would it be *like*?

It would be—*incredible*. He'd used that word and now she found it appropriate as well.

She saw visions of herself helpless and at his mercy. Unable to move, perhaps, or blindfolded, waiting for his touch. Would it be a caress—or maybe even punishment? Would she like that? Would she respond?

Her body gave her the answer. *Hell yeah.*

Licking her lips, Tracy opened her eyes, straightened in her chair and hit the "reply" button. Her fingers were typing out a response almost before she'd thought the words.

Hey George. I got your email. It was...reassuring to know you hadn't just split on me. For a minute there, well yeah, I was nervous. Thanks for putting my mind at ease about that, at least.

And no, I don't think you're a pervert in need of counseling. If you are—well, then I reckon I must be, as well. Because since I read what you wrote, I've done some thinking of my own. I guess I have a different set of rules in my life than you do, because I never get the chance to not be in control of things. That idea is interesting.

I guess I'd need to really trust somebody a lot to hand over that kind of surrender, you know? I'd need to be sure of things like staying safe and not being stupid enough to put myself into a situation that could end up bad for me. But if I did trust him…

Well, I'm not sure. But these ideas, they're ones that I wouldn't say no to exploring. After what we saw tonight – and what we did – maybe we're just hung up on the sex thing. And it was damned good between us, George. You were pretty good yourself. Okay, you were fantastic, but don't get all swelled-headed on me, please?

Where are we going with all this? Who knows? But I will say that a whole bunch of new stuff is going on in my head too. Perhaps…perhaps it might lead to something…

I suppose it's sort of up to you. Or at least we could discuss some options or something…oh hell. This isn't easy, is it?

Anyway, thanks for writing. I appreciate it.

T

With careful deliberation, Tracy checked what she'd written. It sounded…hesitant but encouraging. Which was pretty much how she felt. So—she shrugged and lifted her hand over her mouse. One click and it would be sent.

Perhaps he was in the shower. Or perhaps he was already in bed. In which case he wouldn't get it until the morning anyway. Did it matter? Not particularly.

Tracy breathed in and pressed down on the mouse.

Click.

There. Now she'd gone and done it.

She crawled back onto the mussed bed and curled herself into a ball, tucking her hands beneath her pillow and staring at her laptop, willing the little chime to sound with incoming email.

Wide-eyed and silent, she waited.

* * * * *

George stepped out of the shower. He had just spent a good ten minutes chatting with his penis and discussing the policies of world economics. He knew he was right and doubted his penis's opinion that the world is run by assholes that follow their male anatomy's whims to make policy because pricks rule the world.

As he walked by his computer, dripping on the carpet because he was too lazy to dry off properly, he saw he had incoming mail.

"Oh shit." He knew it was Tracy telling him to go fuck himself. Which technically could be rather difficult.

Carefully he clicked the "open" button and sat down. He began to read her email and a smile widened across his face. His cock also sprang back to life and tried to read the email as well, *really* interested in what was being said and stimulated by the warm flow of blood rushing through it.

George jumped up and in triumphant fashion held his arms up in the air above his head. A casual observer might have been forgiven for assuming he'd just thrown the game-winning touchdown in the last football game of the season. "*Yesssss, yes.*"

He was excited and happy she wasn't freaked out by his open acknowledgement of how she got to him. She was actually *for* it. Finding a woman who wasn't intimidated by the idea of sacrificing control was empowering. It showed a strong level of trust. It was also fucking sexy and arousing as hell.

After toweling off the drips, he decided to reply. Taking a deep breath, he started.

Hello again,

Your friendly neighborhood stalker here.

I am a little hesitant because I haven't been in a situation like this before where I open up so quickly. Last night showed me a side of myself that I haven't seen and it awoke something in me.

That you weren't freaked out was a relief. That you were open to this was a Godsend. If we were face-to-face talking about this I would either be redder than a tomato or stuttering like a schoolboy at a prom.

I don't know how to approach this – if there's an etiquette that I should follow or if I should just dive right in face first. Of course I like diving face first whenever possible. But that's another story.

The nervous George

As he hit "send" he almost crushed the mouse between his fingers. It wasn't the fear of what he had said as much as how he debated that he should maybe tell her these things in person. He'd have to wait until his next email from Tracy. This game of send and wait was driving him crazy.

But fortunately for his sanity, he didn't have to wait long. It seemed that Tracy couldn't sleep either. The response was very quick to arrive in his inbox.

I'm nervous too. This is all new to me. It's something that I'm almost afraid of but can't step away from. We've shared great sex, George. And we've discovered something that interests us both, strictly by chance. I write that yes, I can think about submitting sexually and it turns me on. I guess the fact that I have to be so in control of everything in my life has something to do with it.

I'm tired, probably, tired of making decisions, accepting responsibility – you know how life is. I will say that I'm finding it easier to email you this, since I'm not sure I could have this conversation in person. I have the chance to find the right words, which I probably wouldn't if we were talking about it over drinks or something.

Funny thing is, you remember that picture from the gallery? The one where she was blindfolded and bound, but she was still clearly experiencing a great deal of pleasure? Of course you do – you came out to meet the photographer, didn't you? Sorry. That's how tired I am. I'm forgetting stuff. Well, that picture has stayed in back of my head too. You've brought it out again.

I'm sort of glad you did.

T

George rubbed his hand absently over his face as he absorbed Tracy's words. How to answer her?

Get in here and let me blindfold and fuck *you* into oblivion probably would be a bit too direct, no matter how much he drooled at the thought. He had to play it cool. If he was in control he needed to remain calm. He knew the reason he was attracted to a situation like this was that his life was so regimented and planned out, he had no way of being in control. Here was a chance for him to dominate and be demanding and take the power she would offer to him. George felt the familiar tightness in his pants. It was getting to him again.

His computer dinged once more.

So, assuming you're reading these emails in order, here's my suggestion. I need some sleep so this will be my last one for now. You're interested and I'm interested. Neither of us quite knows where to start, where to go or what to do, but we're definitely interested. I've decided I'm going to ask my friend Eleanor – subtly of course – if she knows of anywhere around here I could get some information. Or even if she knows about that gathering we saw tonight. Perhaps it will be someplace to start.

I don't want to let this go, George. But please don't think I'm being pushy either. It's been a tough few months for me and I'm ready for a change – some fun, some good sex. With you – well, the sex is more than good. I'm looking forward to moving further down that road. Yes, this is pretty damn brazen. But I'm tired and the careful words that should be here – aren't. I liked fucking you. I think you liked it too. Let's do it again. Often.

T

George stared as the words blurred in front of his eyes, blanketed out by the vision of Tracy, naked, crying out as he buried himself to the balls in her. He felt the same way she did – aroused, interested and eager to follow up on whatever it was they'd discovered together.

He leaned to his laptop and sent one last email.

Yes.

Good night.
G.

Chapter Eight

Tracy staggered down to the small dining room the following morning, unable to appreciate the home-like atmosphere radiated by the massive brick fireplace and the overstuffed armchairs ringing the room.

The only thing she wanted to appreciate was about four cups of coffee in rapid succession to help wash down the three aspirins she'd gulped after brushing her teeth. She was still slightly hungover, a bit weak in the knees and had discovered a few odd aches in places that hadn't ached for far too long.

Mixed blessings, all things considered.

"I suppose I couldn't interest you in a nice pot of tea."

The huffy statement emanated from someplace slightly north of her left ear and she turned—carefully—to see the elderly man from the front desk hovering over her.

"Um...just some coffee, Mr. Neville, if you don't mind." She'd remembered his name, thank God.

He looked around him, frowning. "Oh. You mean *me*. Scared me there for a bit with that *Mr. Neville*—I thought the old pater had finally risen from the grave. He was always threatening to, you know. *I'll come back and haunt you, Monty*, he used to say. Wouldn't put it past the old blighter either." He shrugged. "Call me Monty, dear, please. Everybody does."

Tracy gave up on the trying-to-be-polite bit. "Okay, Monty. But if I don't get my coffee soon, I'm not going to be calling anybody anything and you're going to have a semi-comatose woman on your precious Axwooster carpet."

Monty winced. "That's Ax*minster*, dear. I can see I'd better get you that coffee in a hurry. Then we'll see about improving your education on the subject of fine furnishings."

Whatever. Tracy closed her eyes for a second and leaned her chin on her hand, only to be disturbed moments later by Monty placing a surprisingly fragrant pot of coffee next to her cup along with a small pitcher of cream and a sugar bowl.

"Monty, you are a prince among men. Marry me." Tracy chuckled as she poured herself a cup of steaming liquid restorative and sipped appreciatively.

"You couldn't handle me. No stamina, you young things." Monty gazed at her. "Not that it's not a tempting offer, mind you."

Tracy laughed. "Monty…if you have a moment…there's something I'd like to ask you."

He glanced around at the nearly empty room. "Go ahead. I'll try to make room for you in my busy schedule." He pulled up a chair and plunked his butt down with a sigh of pleasure. "Now this is nice. Sharing a spot of breakfast with a lovely woman—warms the cockles of my heart, it does."

"Thank you." Tracy waved his compliment aside.

"I could fix you some food and we could share that too?" He looked hopeful.

"Sorry." Tracy's stomach knotted at the thought of anything solid. "Don't eat in the mornings. But about my question…"

"Single-minded little thing, aren't you?"

This from a man who barely reached her shoulders standing up.

"Nice bit of crunchy bacon? Some toast and marmalade? You know, you remind me a bit of Millicent…" His eyes glazed over.

"Monty." Tracy snapped her fingers under his nose. "Don't drift off on me."

He raised an eyebrow and refocused on her face. "Spoilsport. Go ahead then. Ask me anything, dear. Take advantage of my years of experience. My travels through this amazingly magnificent world we're privileged to inhabit. How I ended up in this travesty of a four-star hotel that barely rates a twinkle in the galactic plan of things…"

"Monty."

"What?"

"Shut *uuuuuuup*."

Monty closed his mouth with a snap and managed to look offended and interested at the same time.

Tracy sighed. "Last night, after dinner, we noticed there were quite a few people here. Well, not *here* precisely, but in that barn place out back."

Monty nodded.

"So we were wondering if it was a party or something?" Tracy didn't want to let him know that she and George had turned into perverts and done the voyeur bit on what was obviously a private gathering.

"And?"

"And what? And nothing. I was just curious, that's all."

Monty's brow went upward once more as he stared at her. "That's *all*?"

"Yes." Tracy finished off her coffee and crossed her arms in front of her defensively. "That's all."

"Hmmm." He continued to stare at her. "Sure you didn't sneak out and take a quick butchers through the window?"

"A quick *what*?"

"Butchers." He paused then shook his head. "Sorry. *Butchers hook. Look.* I forget which side of the big pond I'm on sometimes."

"Oh." Tracy tried to follow his tortured train of thought through the diverse pathways it tended to wander. Her headache threatened to boycott the aspirin.

Pure Sin

"What I'm saying is, I wouldn't be surprised if you peeked in. Saw the party." Monty snickered as Tracy felt the color rise in her cheeks. "I'm right, aren't I? You *naughty* girl, you." He waggled his finger at her.

"Er…well…" She swallowed.

"And then you and that likely lad hopped off back to your room and did a bit of your own partying, didn't you? Can't fool Monty, dear. I know the *look*."

Tracy wanted to bury the *look* in a large hole somewhere close to China along with the rest of her. Unfortunately nothing opened up beneath her, much as she prayed it might. She summoned up her self-control from the soles of her feet and bravely faced him.

"Yes, we did take a quick peek, if you must know. It was…surprising, to say the least of it." *And I'm not telling you anything else, you old bugger.*

"Just a bit of slap-and-tickle, dear. No harm in it. Private party—invitation only. If you hadn't happened to be there at the wrong time, you'd never have known about it, now would you?" Monty looked unperturbed.

"No, I suppose not." She couldn't argue with his logic.

"You know, I was a bit of a dab hand at it myself, back in the old days. Had this riding crop that used to get Millicent all hot and—"

Tracy stood, quickly pushing her chair back with more force than necessary. "Thanks for the coffee, Monty. I really do appreciate it, but unfortunately I have an appointment I don't want to miss. Urgent. Business, you know."

She couldn't even begin to imagine a young Monty walloping somebody named Millicent's bottom with a riding crop. She didn't *want* to. Some things were just better left alone.

"Oh well, I'll tell you about it some other time. Do enjoy yourself, dear. You're a bit skittish this morning, aren't you?" Monty gathered the cups. "That's what happens when you don't start the day with a nice cuppa and a good breakfast. Should have had the bacon...of course, my Millicent—she was skittish too. Especially when I'd get those knickers off her..."

Tracy turned and damn near ran for the door.

* * * * *

Eleanor was waiting for Tracy, a smile on her face and a hand on her round stomach. "C'mon in. I'm sorry about yesterday. This little fella seems to want to give me a hard time in the afternoons. Contrary little devil—just like his father." She grinned at Tracy.

The two women hugged and Tracy settled comfortably on the kitchen chair, refusing to do the more formal living room thing. "I'm not my mother. I'm happier here." She grinned at Eleanor. "More like our dorm room."

Eleanor shuddered. "God, I hope not."

The conversation ranged back over college memories, moved on to Eleanor's marriage to Justin—who still sounded like a combination of a Greek god and a movie star—and finally to the present and the reason Tracy was here in the first place.

"So. Purett's Inn." Tracy smiled. "Or as the sign so picturesquely puts it—*Pure Sin*."

Eleanor chuckled. "Yeah, I noticed that myself." She reached for her green tea. "What do you think?"

Tracy considered the question. "It has definite potential. Delightful architecture that looks like a good coat of fresh paint wouldn't come amiss. From the outside it'll have a lot of eye appeal to the new visitor. Charm in abundance...that sort of thing."

Eleanor nodded. "It is quaint. Very old-world." She sipped. "Go on."

"The facilities need updating." Tracy rotated her shoulders as she organized her thoughts. "The rooms are a fair size, not large but manageable. I wouldn't go knocking walls down or anything. But the plumbing definitely needs a facelift. Old-world is all well and good, but not when it comes to bathrooms."

"Agreed."

"I'd recommend expanding the dining room a bit. There's a couple of smaller rooms I think, on the ground floor, that don't serve much of a useful purpose. People don't read the papers over their tea anymore—although God knows Monty probably does—" She ignored Eleanor's spurt of laughter. "So those smaller rooms could be absorbed into the dining room and possibly convert the entire thing into a nice little restaurant with a wine bar attached for guests or something."

Eleanor's gaze remained on her face. "Okay. I'm with you so far."

Tracy cleared her throat. "There's a big barn sort of structure in back."

"Yes, there is."

"Apparently they have private parties there?"

Innocently, Eleanor tilted her head. "Do they?"

Tracy watched her friend and recognized the glint in her eyes. "Damn you, Eleanor. You know *exactly* what I'm talking about."

Eleanor burst out laughing, then stopped, looked panicked and dashed from the room only to return a few minutes later. "Sorry. I have to be careful when I laugh." She glanced at Tracy. "Don't ask."

"I won't. Believe me." There were things about pregnancy Tracy was quite happy to *not* know. "But you know I'm going to ask about those people I saw last night."

"Ooooh." Eleanor's eyes widened. "You peeked?"

"I didn't *peek*." Tracy was mildly offended that everybody in this town assumed she was some sort of Peeping Tom. "I simply happened to see in through one of the windows."

After moving a convenient crate to the right position and climbing all over George.

Eleanor let it go. "Well, at least now you know." She leaned back. "Here's the skinny, Trace. Purett's Inn is a meeting place for adults interested in consensual activities that are slightly outside the norm, as you may have gathered. They don't violate any ordinances—I don't think—because it's private property and the parties are by invitation only." She wrinkled her nose. "I never got invited. I don't think Justin would allow it, the bum."

Tracy digested this information. "Go on."

"Well, it turns out that Mike, one of the guys who works for Justin, has come into some money. He's into that scene—the whole bondage thing—with his girlfriend Amy. He asked me if I thought the inn would be a good investment, with the possibility of promoting it to that section of the vacationing adult public. I don't know who has the title, but apparently Mike knows and could buy himself a sizeable percentage if he wanted. His concerns are that it's going to lose him money the way it stands right now."

Tracy nodded. Mike sounded like he had his head on straight.

"Mike's thinking that some delicately phrased promotion in the right places would attract like-minded…er…"

"Fetish folk?" Tracy tried not to giggle.

"That'll do." Eleanor grinned. "I guess there aren't a lot of places for them to gather and swap…um…spanking techniques or whatever it is they do when they get together. I'm not sure." She blinked coyly up at Tracy from under her eyelashes. "Do you? Did you see anything…*interesting*?"

Tracy looked at Eleanor and then looked at her pregnant stomach. Nope. She wasn't about to share anything that might induce early labor.

She shook her head. "Not much other than some leather and studs. You know, just what you'd expect."

"Oh." Eleanor seemed disappointed. Then she shrugged. "Anyway, you've got the general idea. I told Mike I'd invite you down here and if you think the idea is worth considering, then I'll send you over to meet him." She drained her tea with a grimace. "God, that stuff tastes like shit. I'd kill for coffee sometimes. The only drawback to this whole process."

Tracy smiled with only half her attention. The other half was busily whirling through possibilities for the inn. She had a business plan half written in her head when she realized Eleanor was quietly munching on carrot sticks and watching her think.

"You like the idea, don't you?"

Did she? Tracy thought about that. "I think I do." She toyed with her coffee cup, which—thankfully—contained coffee, not that green slurp Eleanor was drinking. "May I ask you something?"

"Sure. Go ahead."

Carefully, Tracy chose her words. "This whole bondage scene. The sexual domination thing—what do you think of it?"

Eleanor crunched thoughtfully. "Well—I think it's fine."

"You do?"

"Sure. Consenting adults can do whatever they want, honey. We're out of the Victorian era, you know."

Tracy snorted. "I know that. And *you* know that's not what I mean."

Eleanor giggled. "You want to know if I think it's…um…erotic?"

Tracy swallowed and nodded. "Yeah."

"Well…" Eleanor contemplated a carrot. "Yes, I do think it could be a turn-on. Let's face it, ninety percent of couples have probably done something that could be termed bondage in one form or another." She glanced at Tracy. "And the other ten percent are lying."

"You think?"

"Definitely. A tie? The belt from a bathrobe? C'mon, Trace. It adds a little something." She leaned forward. "Look, as I understand it, anything that intensifies the sex is good. And there's a lot of people out there with stressful lives who simply adore the idea of letting it all go for a little while. Letting somebody else call the shots. It sounds good to me. In fact…" She paused.

"No. Please. I don't want to know." Tracy held her hands over her ears as Eleanor laughed.

"It's okay. I'm not sharing intimate details of my sex life, even with you, honey. But I will say that Justin and I share a healthy relationship. Sometimes that relationship goes down slightly different paths than just plain old vanilla sex."

"Vanilla? Sex comes in flavors now?"

Eleanor laughed again. "It's a term Mike uses for those people who keep it simple. From what I understand, his interests are *not* vanilla. But don't confuse the occasional blindfold with true BDSM."

"Er…okay. I won't." Tracy was getting more confused by the minute.

"Look, you really ought to talk to Mike. He knows a helluva lot more stuff than I ever could. Or ever want to, come to think of it. You should go by the bar. I think he's there today."

The phone rang and Eleanor glanced at the clock. "Ooh, I almost forgot. Gimme a minute." She levered herself from her chair and went to answer the phone, leaving Tracy to her muddled thoughts.

Apparently she wasn't weird, just ready to surrender control to somebody else in bed. And apparently it wasn't that unusual.

The facts made her feel a little better about herself and the added endorsement that came with Eleanor's non-confession also eased her mind. So getting kinky with George really wasn't *that* kinky in the overall scheme of things.

Then she remembered the woman with the collar and the leash. *Uh uh.* No leash for this gal. She'd submit in bed, but that would be as far as it would go. George had better understand *that* right from the get-go.

But oddly enough, Tracy knew he would understand. He wouldn't need an instruction sheet or a list of do's and don'ts. Somehow she was convinced they were both on the same page when it came to sexual submission. He would accept it and use it to make her eyes roll.

It was odd how sure she was, since they'd really only met such a short time ago…

"Sorry. That was my sister Jodi. You didn't meet her yet, did you?" Eleanor lumbered back. "She just got back in town. She and her man have been traveling."

Tracy smiled. "That's nice. I haven't seen her since your wedding. You must be happy she's home."

"I am. And she's ecstatic about being an aunt soon, not to mention that guy of hers. Marcus. He's a hunk and a half."

Tracy blinked. "Marcus?"

"Yep. Marcus works for Justin. He tends bar. Lovely man."

"That's odd." Tracy stared at Eleanor. "I met this guy George. We'd run into each other a little while ago in town and he's here as well, staying at the inn. He's here to find a photographer he knows by the name of Marcus."

"Damn. Small world—Marcus is a fabulous photographer." Eleanor leaned back and rubbed the base of her spine. "I'll bet they're one and the same. How about that?" She paused. "You met this guy named George?"

"Er, yes."

Eleanor bit her lip. "You know him?"

"Yes."

"Would that be in the biblical sense?" Eleanor's mouth quivered.

"Don't you dare laugh. He's really nice. Hell on wheels in bed too."

"*Tracy Harmon*. You *slept* with him? After knowing him for what—five minutes? His name is *George*?"

"Yeah." Tracy started to giggle. "George Cluny."

Eleanor's jaw dropped. "You're kidding."

"Nope. But it's spelled C-L-U-N-Y. And yes, I...well, we didn't exactly sleep much. And it was more than five minutes. We met in town a couple of months ago."

"You dated?"

"Not exactly." Tracy swallowed. "We said hello to each other and sort of chatted."

"For how long?"

"Well, okay. Five minutes or so. But it was an intense five minutes, El. Honest."

"Holy shit. This is not like you. Whatever happened to Simon the sleaze?"

"He was a mistake that lasted way too long."

"George isn't?"

Tracy paused. "God, I hope not."

Eleanor shook her head. "I still can't believe you slept with him so soon."

"Hey." Tracy frowned. "This isn't the Victorian era, ya know." She threw Eleanor's words right back at her. "I'm over twenty-one. So is he. We're consenting adults—we both found something we like in the other—what more can I say?"

Eleanor thought about that for a moment. "You really like him, huh?"

There was silence, a long silence while Tracy chewed over the question. Finally she drew a breath. "Yes. There's something about him that I find—appealing. I don't know what it is. He makes me laugh. He listens to me. He *gets* me. That's about the only way I can express it."

"I'd say he's *got* you. Or had you. Or whatever." Eleanor smiled. "But hey, who am I to criticize? Justin had me hot and bothered after our first dance together. And I was doing terribly awful and wonderful things to him shortly thereafter." Her grin was as wicked as any Tracy had ever seen on the face of a pregnant woman.

"Well, leaving that subject alone, I guess I need to go talk to this Mike person. He's at the bar?" Tracy eagerly shifted gears into more comfortable areas of conversation.

"Should be. You know where it is?"

"Yeah. George and I were there last night. I wonder if we saw him?" She shrugged. "I'll introduce myself this time around. See what's happening with him and what exactly it is he wants to do." She gathered her things.

"Okay. And let's get together again, maybe tomorrow. It's Sunday. Jodi and Marcus will be here."

"If I can, I will. Promise." Tracy carefully hugged Eleanor. "You go take a nap or knit something. Whatever moms-to-be do."

Eleanor laughed. "Only if you promise to tell me more of your adventures. I live pretty much vicariously at the moment."

"We'll see."

* * * * *

"I'm not shitting you, Justin, honest. The woman had a contraption on her mouth that made it stay open. Kinda like a donut. There are times when one of those babies would come in handy to keep a woman quiet."

"Like on Sundays during the playoffs?"

"Damn straight." George nodded.

He'd come to The Mating Place looking for Marcus, who was apparently due back there any minute. In the meantime, he'd struck up a conversation with Justin who was only too ready to take a break from checking the books.

"I'm not into that kind of thing myself, but it *is* pretty interesting. To have total control over someone else. That knowledge that they'll do whatever you ask. Whatever it is. I envy that. I am so pussy-whipped. I lost any control when I said *I do*." Justin grinned.

"Personally, I wouldn't be complaining. Your wife is gorgeous. That red hair, that body? You're a lucky man." George glanced again at the photo of Eleanor that Justin had tacked to the wall behind the bar.

"I know. I'm going to have to talk her into a little bit of that stuff you're talking about. You know, spice up things. Of course that would be *after* the baby's born. Don't want to be poking the kid in the forehead over and over."

"Just hope she doesn't get one of those willie clamps. That thing was fucking scary."

Both guys squeezed their legs together as they contemplated that thought.

"I need a drink." George's words came from the heart.

Justin pulled two beers from behind the counter and twisted the tops off. "I'll join you. My treat."

"Just like Marcus to be late. That guy was always a step behind. But the women he used to hook up with? You wouldn't believe it. There were these twins we knew. Two of the hottest girls you could imagine. He had both of them eating out of his hands. It was bad enough they both flashed him their tits at the bar he was working at, but then he took them back to his apartment and took pictures of them *both* naked."

"Sounds like Marcus." Justin smiled. "He does love that camera of his."

"The asshole wouldn't show me the pictures either. Said it was something private they asked him to do. Lucky bastard. But he did okay. He ended up with that model, Vanessa something-or-other and she was *hot*. Kind of a bitch but she was…*holy crap*."

"What?" Justin followed George's line of sight, trying to see what he saw.

There was a woman's shadow on a step stool. "You see the ass on that babe?"

"Yep, she works next door. That's Jodi."

George stared as Jodi stepped down and bent over to rummage through the box she had pulled off the top shelf. She was wearing tight jeans and a cropped T-shirt, kinda like the girl next door.

George swallowed. This Jodi sure knew how to present herself as the girl you'd love to live next door to.

She looked over to Justin and waved. Then her gaze turned toward George, sending an instant rush of excitement to fill his mind while his blood rushed to fill something else.

After blinking a few times George spoke. "You see how that woman looked at me? Shit, if I could figure out a way to *save* that…sex in a bottle, dude. I'd make a frickin' fortune."

Justin looked past George and shook his head.

"I wonder…I mean I just started seeing Tracy but I've always had an itch for a threesome…"

"Scratch your itch someplace else. She isn't into threes. Of course you're probably talking about the three inches in your pants." The deep voice from behind him made George's neck hair stand on end.

"You son of a bitch." George grinned, knowing he was busted.

Turning on his stool, he stared at a wide chest. Looking up, he saw a shit-eating grin on his old friend's face.

"Been a long time, George."

"It sure has, Marcus. How ya been?" They shook hands and Marcus walked around to his standard bartender spot.

"I know exactly the right drink for George. *The Usual*."

"Oh hell no! I haven't had one of those in years—not since that gay bar incident."

Justin raised an eyebrow and looked at George. "Gay bar incident?"

"Marcus never told you?" George took a deep breath. "This asshole made this drink called *The Usual* for us to have at parties—it got us and our female companions hammered. Well, Mr. Nice Guy here got me totally wasted on them one night, took me to a gay bar and had one of the guys pretend to be my date. I was so drunk I couldn't tell. Until of course I was kissing the guy and reached down between his legs. The fucker had a bigger dick than mine."

"Oh come on, George, I didn't tell you to French kiss the guy. I just…well, I'll admit that was kind of a shitty thing to do to a friend. But it was real funny and the pictures were hilarious." Marcus paused dramatically. "You still have that guy's phone number?"

"Enough about me, how are you doing?" George knew it was definitely time to change the subject.

"Can't complain. Been working here with Justin for about three years. Nice place."

Justin interrupted. "He's also been dating my sister-in-law Jodi."

"You mean that fine brunette is your *sister-in-law*?"

"Yep." Justin smirked. "Fine-ness runs in Eleanor's family."

George blinked. "So *that's* your new girlfriend, huh, Marcus?"

"Well, not exactly." Marcus looked a bit self-conscious. "She's my fiancée after this weekend."

Justin fumbled his beer, nearly emptying the glass onto the floor. "Did you say *fiancée*?"

Calmly Marcus reached beneath the bar and grabbed a beer for himself along with a replacement for Justin. "Yes.

Why do you think we took the weekend off? I wanted to take her somewhere romantic—you know, someplace I could pop the question the right way."

Justin grinned. "I thought you weren't the marrying kind."

"Hey, at some point you have to start growing up. Believing in the dream that there really is someone there for you."

George watched, fascinated, as Marcus developed that blank sort of stare men tend to get when thinking of love and cuddles.

Then he looked at Justin. Justin looked back at George. They both turned back to look at Marcus.

"Riiiiight." Three voices spoke simultaneously, a choir of testosterone.

"I'm actually surprised I can still walk. That woman's an animal when she gets excited." Marcus paused and grinned. "Oh by the way…she said yes."

Justin slapped him on the back. "Congrats, Marcus. I'm really happy for you."

"You probably won't be for long. Jodi's gonna have Eleanor involved up to her eyeballs in planning the wedding." He snickered. "Guess who's helping to foot the bill?"

"Great news, Marcus. I'm happy for you too." George held up his beer. "Cheers."

The three guys all clinked their bottles together and took a drink.

"Oh Justin—Eleanor called looking for you. She's sending a friend of hers over. Wants her to meet Mike for some reason." Marcus passed along the message.

"I'd better go call her. Nice meeting you, George." Justin smacked Marcus on the back again as he passed. "Well, we're losing another man to the other side. Welcome to the pussy-whipped club, buddy."

After he'd gone, the two remaining men sat talking and catching up on lost time. They didn't see much of each other but their bullshit still flowed like the old days.

"They were identical twins? In *every* way?" George looked at Marcus, almost salivating at his story.

"I don't know, George. It was a photo shoot and they wanted it to be sent to a magazine." Marcus grinned. "You haven't changed a bit."

"You know I always had a thing for twins." George paused. "Anyway, I came here for more than just catching up."

"I figured. What do you need?" Marcus smiled.

George shook his head "Uh uh. I don't need anything. I was at an art show in the city with my ex-girlfriend a little while back. There was this picture—hell—it was fucking *art*. It was of a woman, bound and sitting in this odd chair, with a guy in front of her. It had your name on it and I wanted to buy it to put it in my house. Well, more like put it in my bedroom, to be honest."

"I know the one. But I can't sell it."

"What? Why not?" George looked puzzled.

"It's not mine to sell. I took those shots for a friend." Marcus sipped his beer and continued. "The exhibit you went to—the art dealer there had to ask Mike if he could use some of that photo art and Mike gave him the okay to show it."

"Mike?"

"Yeah, the guy in the picture. It's him and his girlfriend. I took that shot about a year ago."

"Shit. I really wanted to get that. I met this woman, Tracy, when I was looking at it and it really got to her. Fucking thing got to me too. That was *hot*."

"You can ask Mike if he wants to sell it."

"I can?"

"Sure, he works for Justin here at the bar. He's probably loading stock from the trucks in the back right now."

Chapter Nine

Tracy carefully climbed up the steps to the loading dock behind The Mating Place and peered inside. "Hello? Mike?"

"I'm over here." A man stepped from behind a pile of boxes. "Can I help you?"

She smiled. "Hi. I'm Tracy Harmon, Eleanor's friend. I think she told you I was coming?"

"Oh yeah, hello, Ms. Harmon. Nice to meet you." He wiped his hands on his jeans and extended one, which Tracy dutifully shook. Then he glanced around. "I don't have an office, and I guess we can't really talk here…" A truck roared past making that fact quite plain. "Would you like to come in to our break room? It's not much, but at least it's quiet."

"Sure." Tracy nodded and followed him through a door into a small but functional room with a table, several chairs, a coffee urn and a microwave oven. There was a tiny fridge beneath one counter from which Mike pulled a bottle of water. "Would you like some?"

She shook her head. "No, I'm fine, thanks." She moved a chair near the table and sat down. "Do you have a few minutes to spare me? I have a couple of questions about the inn."

"Yeah, now's good. I'm due for a break." He grinned. "Justin isn't about to fire me if I run over a bit. I do the grunt work he hates."

She smiled back. Mike was older than he looked but still very young to her way of thinking. Probably no more than his mid-twenties. His T-shirt sported the logo of a hot rock band and his jeans had the obligatory rip or two in the knees. Sneakers and a tousled haircut completed the still-in-college look—surprising Tracy.

"So." She folded her hands in front of her and rested them on the table. "Eleanor tells me you're considering Purett's Inn as an investment opportunity."

Mike nodded. "More than that. I'd like to buy a sufficient interest in the property to assure an income and possibly locate a small residence there for myself. That would help with the cash flow, of course, even though it would reduce my profits. But the consequent reduction in my personal overhead would probably offset that loss. Rents these days..." He grimaced.

Tracy blinked. *Note to self. Do not underestimate Mike's financial acuity.*

"Yes. Well." She gathered her thoughts. "Those are matters you're going to want to discuss with your accountant. I'm here to give you some of my thoughts on promoting the inn, possibly establishing a website, that sort of thing."

Mike took a long drink of water. "Yep. It's the age of cyber advertising. If we can't sell the inn on the Internet as an appealing destination—" He lifted his eyebrows. "I'm screwed."

Tracy inclined her head. "Agreed. However, from what I've seen so far, I don't see that as happening immediately. The place has a lot to recommend it." She paused and lowered her gaze to her hands. "Correct me if I'm wrong, but I understand that you would consider marketing the place to a...a...certain...um...clientele?"

Mike nodded. "The adult-oriented sector. Yes."

"Right. The adult sector." Tracy cleared her throat. "In the interests of total disclosure here, Mike, I should tell you that a friend and I happened to notice the...er...*meeting* that was taking place there last night."

"Meeting?" Mike looked puzzled for a minute, then his expression cleared. "Oh, you mean the dungeon."

Tracy felt the color rise in her cheeks. "Yes. The dungeon."

"Good. Then you know about the BDSM activities. They've become pretty regular and very popular. I see them as a strong market possibility." Mike gazed at her, quite unruffled by her disclosures.

She cleared her throat. "Yes. I suppose so." She fiddled with the catch on her purse.

"Ms. Harmon, how much do you know about the BDSM scene?"

"Honestly?" She looked at him. "Little to nothing."

Mike watched her, a little too closely for her comfort. "Something tells me you're not completely uninterested?"

"I…er…"

He interrupted her. "Let me ask you a question. Were you alone last night when you saw the dungeon?"

"Um, no. Not exactly."

Mike nodded. "And would you say you found it—you *both* found it—*arousing*?"

Tracy gulped. "You could say that, yes."

He leaned back in his chair. "Good. That response is not unusual. Now imagine a vacationer looking for just that. A place to enjoy his or her pursuits amongst like-minded friends. Somewhere private, somewhere an *interested* party can explore this scene without fear of recrimination or condemnation."

Tracy nodded, understanding his point. "I see." She thought for a moment. "How big is this…um…scene?"

He spread his hands wide. "Huge, Ms. Harmon. And growing steadily. Every day more and more people find themselves fascinated—and aroused—by the possibilities offered through Domination and submission. Most are sexually aroused. Others find the process mentally stimulating. Whatever their needs or their particular desires, the BDSM scene is expanding to include greater numbers of practitioners daily. Folks like yourself who have discovered the possibilities…"

"Really?" Tracy couldn't help the question. "That many? Enough in this area to fill the inn?"

"Twice over if we put the word out properly. Right now, the inn can't handle that number of guests. People have to stay elsewhere or simply drive over for the fun. You've seen it. It needs work—quite a bit of work. I just need to know that it *will* be worth it, worth making that kind of investment. And obviously that we can make sure potential guests know about it."

The conversation turned to more practical matters, relieving Tracy's heated cheeks for a little while as they discussed cost-effective improvements and the possibility of website development and hosting.

But eventually Mike returned to the crux of the matter. "So. Tell me. How exciting did you find last night's activities?"

She took a breath. "Is that relevant?"

Mike's eyes remained steadily on her face. He never moved, just watched her and waited.

It came to her suddenly. Mike was a *Dominant*.

She shifted a little under the weight of his gaze. "If you must know, yes, I found it all very fascinating and my curiosity about this whole Dominant-submissive thing was…aroused."

"Good." He nodded as a door at the back of the room opened and two men entered.

"Hey, Mike."

"Marcus."

"Tracy?"

"*George*?" Tracy's head swiveled as the names popped across the room like fireworks.

"This is Tracy?" A tall man blinked at her.

George nodded. "Yeah, Marcus. This is Tracy."

"Marcus? *The* Marcus?" Tracy pointed at him.

He rolled his eyes. "I'm out of here before somebody turns this into a musical comedy." He turned to leave. "Mike, this is my college buddy George. Who knows Tracy. Who knows you. I don't know *anybody*. I'm gone."

His departure left the three remaining people looking at each other in confusion.

Tracy found her voice. "This is a surprise, George. I didn't expect to find you here."

"I was looking for Marcus. Turns out that Mike here owns that photo I wanted."

"Photo?" Mike looked at George. "What photo?"

"Oh God. The *photo*." Tracy moaned and sank back in her chair.

"Saw it in a gallery in town, Mike. A woman, bound, with a guy…um…in front of her." George coughed a little. "If you catch my drift."

Mike snapped his fingers and crossed to a row of lockers, opening the end one. "You mean *this* photo?"

And there it was, the woman bound and blindfolded, the man's cock deep in her mouth.

Tracy bit back a groan of embarrassment. This wasn't a moment to remind the two men that she was even in the room, let alone looking at the photo taped to Mike's locker.

"Yeah." George looked at it in admiration. "That's the one. If I could, I would have bought it on the spot." He glanced at Mike. "I saw the credit and recognized Marcus' name. It's a masterpiece. I figured it was worth taking a few days to chase it down and touch base with him while I was at it."

"Glad you like it. Amy and I enjoyed that shoot, I must admit."

Tracy emitted a sort of strangled gasp that caught in her tonsils. "That's *you*?" Her question came out as a squeak.

"Yes." Mike smiled. "And my girlfriend."

"You squeaked." George smirked at Tracy.

"Did not."

"Did too."

"I..." Tracy looked at George and then remembered where she was. She closed her mouth with a snap.

Mike chuckled. "Seems like you two need to get your roles straight. Exactly who's dominating who here?"

Tracy swore she could hear the bones crack in George's neck as his head jerked from the photo to Mike. "Dominate? Who said anything about dominate?"

"She did." Mike pointed at Tracy.

"I..." *Oh fuck.* The color flooded hotly back into her cheeks.

"She did?" George raised an eyebrow.

"Look." Mike took pity on Tracy. "Perhaps this would be a lot easier if you two worked it out together. Without me."

Tracy stood, ignoring the sweat that threatened to soak her armpits. "That's a very sensible suggestion, Mike."

"Here's another." Mike leaned in to his locker and pulled out an envelope from which he removed two cardboard keys. "These will admit you to the dungeon today. This afternoon is a small affair—vendors mostly, offering tools and toys for playtime. This evening—well, more of what you glimpsed last night. But this time you can come inside and experience everything up close." He closed the locker. "Interested?"

* * * * *

George watched as Tracy took the keys from Mike's hand then turned her head to look at him, a question in her eyes.

"George? What do *you* think?"

Mike smiled and didn't give George a chance to answer. "Doors open at eight for the dungeon events. My girlfriend Amy will be there. I'll tell her to look out for you, Ms. Harmon." He turned to George. "And you—if you should see a tall man with a bit of grey in his hair, that's Master Damien.

Say hello. He'll answer any questions for you. The man's a whiz at helping folks."

"How will Amy know who I am?" Tracy sounded uncertain as she passed one of the keys to George.

Mike chuckled. "You bring any leather or studs with you?"

"Er, no."

"She'll find you." Mike sounded quite definite.

"Okay then." George swallowed, looking at the cardboard cutout in his hand. "Eight it is."

"I have to go. Things to do, you know." Tracy gathered her purse and fussed in it for her keys. "Mike, I have a couple of appointments with realtors this afternoon. I'm going to research the current market around this area. Get a feel for the place, for the kind of residents it attracts and the costs involved in construction. That sort of thing."

For some reason, George sensed she was nervous. God knew he wasn't sure what to expect, but he didn't really feel nervous, just pleasantly excited at the prospect of actually going inside a real honest-to-God dungeon.

With Tracy.

"Okay." Mike opened the door to the loading dock. "You know your way from here, yes?"

"Yes. I'm fine. George, I'll see you tonight. Around eight-ish. Okay? Bye."

"Tracy, I…"

Mike caught his arm before George could follow her. "Let her go, man. It's okay. She's got a lot on her mind right now."

"She does?"

"Yeah. If she's really interested in being your sub—your submissive—she's got to give herself the chance to understand what that means. You need to give her time."

"Uhhhh—okay."

Mike slapped him on the shoulder. "Relax. It'll be fine. I have a good feeling about the two of you. I wouldn't have given you invitations otherwise. Sure I need Ms. Harmon to give me some business advice, and you're a friend of Marcus', which is good enough for me. But still—sometimes this kind of relationship works, sometimes it doesn't. I'm thinking that for you two it will work."

George shook his head. "I wish I was as sure as you are."

"Don't sweat it. Let it happen naturally. I gotta go back to work now." He turned away. "Remember—Master Damien."

George nodded. "Damien. Hey wasn't that the kid in that movie about . . ."

"See ya."

George was left alone with his thoughts. Sub? Dominant? Suddenly it all seemed a bit too real.

I need another beer.

And maybe some leather pants?

The thought of the vendor exhibition darted into George's mind. Why not go over and check it out? See what sort of toys were out there? What the options were? Tracy said she had appointments that afternoon. She'd be gone for a couple of hours at least, so he was free to do as he pleased.

He would have been even more pleased if they could've fucked their way through the afternoon, but some things just weren't meant to be. Not right at that moment, anyway.

He strolled back through the bar and waved at Marcus who was putting the last of the new bottles on the shelves behind the bar. "Later, buddy."

"Hey. Wanna go grab some lunch?" Marcus finished his task and wiped his hands on a towel. "I've got a couple of hours to kill. My woman's dumped me for her sister—I guess they're starting all that wedding planning stuff. I need to hang with a guy for a bit." He grinned. "Get my macho fix before it's too late."

"Sure." George sadly acknowledged to himself he had nothing better to do. Fucking Tracy would have been better, of course, *but...* He sighed. "They got any of those gut-busting-burrito places around here?"

"No way! You and burritos don't mix. I remember the parties and you lighting your farts on fire. Let's go next door. Even though Jodi's out, the food is real good."

George remembered as he stepped out of The Mating Place and into The Eating Place that he'd clean forgotten to ask Mike about getting a print of that photo.

Hell. Then he realized that if he played his cards right — he might not need it. There was a strong possibility he might just have the real McCoy.

* * * * *

Tracy really did have an appointment with a realtor. It took less than ten minutes, but had been the first excuse she could grab to get the hell out of Dodge. Or, to translate that stupid phrase, get the hell away from the man who made her break out in even more of a sweat than her conversation with Mike.

Oh fuck it all.

She was seriously in lust with George Cluny. She leaned against her car after leaving the realty office and laughed at herself. Saying it out loud would probably bring her a chorus of agreement from any woman under the age of eighty within earshot.

Saying it *silently* gave it a whole different meaning. *Her* George disturbed her on so many levels she nearly got seasick just thinking about him. When he'd walked into the lunchroom with his friend Marcus, her body had tingled from crotch to earlobes with awareness, a pure and simple sexual heat that flashed through her body, catching her unawares.

It had never happened before. She'd never sweat like that, either beneath her arms or between her legs. He made her nerve endings dance to a rapid salsa beat, her heart thud irregularly and her toes itch.

It had to be lust. Honest, uncomplicated lust. Toss in the hint of domination and the pot was well and truly on its way to boiling. The pot, in this case, being her pussy.

She drove slowly back to the inn, doing her best not to rack up a serious traffic violation even though her thoughts were anywhere but on the road. Finally she parked in the lot, wheels scrunching over the gravel and coming to a halt.

In the silence that followed the removal of the ignition key, Tracy sat there—and thought.

Round and round, her thoughts revolved in odd whirling patterns, always returning to the notion of sexual submission. What did it truly entail? Why were so many people enamored of this idea? What would she get out of it, if anything? Sure, she and George had played around with the notion. Lightheartedly, she'd offered to be his slave. The consequent sex had been sublime.

Now they were taking another step into the more formalized world of BDSM. A world where one partner would dominate the other completely. Where she would truly become George's slave and he would become her Master.

Sort of.

And in a lightning-fast change of thought, she wondered what the hell she was supposed to *wear* to a dungeon. She certainly had no clue what was considered acceptable attire and to judge from what she'd seen last night, clothing might well be optional.

Okay. Naked isn't me. Not in a public place, anyway. It's that cellulite thing.

She put her keys into her bag and opened the car door, realizing as she did so that there were a lot more cars there— just like last night. Apparently these were the invited guests who wanted to shop at the vendor event.

And who, in their right mind, *wouldn't* want to shop such an event? Not Tracy. Without a second thought she reached into her bag for the pass. She had no idea where George was, but doubted he'd be interested in this side of things anyway. Guys and shopping…not the best mix.

Bravely she clutched the key and marched up to the barn door. Soon-to-be-submissive woman on a mission. She would scope out the tools of the trade and maybe pick up a few tips while she was at it.

Heart thumping fast beneath her neat blouse, Tracy pushed open the door and stepped inside.

Chapter Ten
ഗ

The first thing that struck her was how small the space was, compared to what she thought she'd seen through the window.

The wooden floor glowed in the light of the sun, which streamed in through unshaded windows, and the walls were shining too, varnished to a smooth finish. Then Tracy realized that a good portion of the barn was curtained off, a dark brown heavy drape separating the vendors' area from the rest of the space. There were a dozen or so tables arranged along the walls and curtains, some simple layouts, others with racks behind them also showing off their wares.

Curious as to what was for sale, Tracy turned right and gasped aloud. The very first table she saw was almost covered with the softest pile of fur she'd ever seen. Automatically her hand reached out.

"That had better be clean." A stern voice froze Tracy's arm.

She looked at the woman who had risen from behind the table. "It is. Promise." Tracy held up her palms for inspection.

The woman relaxed. "Sorry. Reflex action. I have three boys with a taste for chips and a bad habit of wiping their hands on whatever's near. Including my furs."

Tracy laughed. "That would be a sin indeed if they came near these beauties."

There must have been close to twenty pieces of fur lying neatly next to each other on the dark cloth, ranging in shades from almost pure white to the darkest grey tipped with silver.

"Fox tails. Aren't they lovely?"

"Mmm." Tracy caressed one, loving the almost insubstantial whisper of the fur as it drifted across her fingers. "What are they used for?"

"They're floggers."

Tracy blinked. "Floggers? How can you flog somebody with something this soft?"

The woman chuckled. "You don't. You use the *other* end." She picked one up, showing Tracy the leather-covered handle. On one end was the fox tail, on the other a bundle of long leather thongs.

"Oh my. Clever." Tracy stared at it. "How does it work?"

"Like this." The woman rotated her wrist with all the skill of a prize-winning baton twirler. She set up a rhythm that thudded the leather against the surface of the table, smoothly punishing the inoffensive cloth with firm lashes.

"Wow. You're good." Tracy watched with awe.

"Takes practice." The woman looked pleased and stopped the demonstration. "Then, when the sub's ass is all nice and rosy, you stroke it—with this." She rubbed the fox tail gently over Tracy's arm. "Nice, huh?"

"Beautiful. Thanks for showing me."

"My pleasure." The woman nodded as Tracy moved on. Floggers looked like a skill that needed to be learned. She wasn't ready to learn *that* yet. She also hoped George wasn't either. A spank or two was one thing. A flogging was another.

The next table featured more floggers, single-ended this time, featuring colored lashes and an assortment of cuffs designed to match. The totally coordinated submissive obviously wouldn't want to live without a set. Ditto the larger cuffs that were displayed around a set of mannequin thighs and held apart by a sort of bar affair. Where the rest of the mannequin was…that was anybody's guess.

Tracy admired the workmanship and moved on, confessing to the salesman that the intricacies of Turk's Head knotting techniques was way beyond her ability to comprehend. He seemed disappointed but smiled anyway.

There were several other visitors strolling around, but overall it was quiet. Perhaps because she'd gotten there early. She walked quite rapidly past the table featuring leather collars, leashes, leather wrist bands and—astoundingly—a leather thong designed for men. All sporting large metal studs. As did the skimpy leather bra.

Er – no thanks.

Likewise the next table, tucked into one corner. Tracy looked—and then looked again. Yes, those really were adult diapers. Right next to the oversized baby's bottle, the enormous pacifier and the really frightening baby bonnets.

Tracy sooo didn't want to know anything about this table or its customers.

But the next one did catch her interest. At first glance it looked like an assortment of surgical instruments or artists' tools. She moved nearer.

"Amazing, aren't they?" The young woman seated behind the table noticed Tracy's intent scrutiny.

"Yes indeed. What are they?"

There was a low laugh. "You're new, huh. These are Wartenburg wheels."

"They look like tiny spurs…" Tracy touched one of the little implements with a fingertip.

"They do, you're right." She looked up. "I'm Janie. You coming to the dungeon tonight?"

"I think so, yes." Tracy swallowed.

"Oh cool. It'll be a lot of fun. And these wheels are always popular. Can't keep 'em in stock."

"Er…what does one *do* with them?" Tracy's curiosity got the better of her.

Janie leaned her elbows on the table and arranged the devices in even rows. "Well, they're really interesting things.

Originally they were used as neurological tools. Still are, I believe. The doctor would run one over a patient's sensitive spots to judge the extent of nerve damage." She picked up one of the shiny tools. Its handle was about six inches long and at one end was a little wheel with sharp spokes set to spin freely around its axis. "Here, give me your arm."

Tracy held out her arm obediently and Janie ran the wheel up the inside over her ticklish skin.

"Ooooh." She blinked. "It doesn't hurt at all, does it? Just sort of stings a little..."

"Yeah." Janie giggled. "Cool sensation, isn't it? Imagine that on your nipples — or better yet, your clit."

Tracy gulped. "Uhh...well...maybe I'll hold that thought for a bit."

"Sure thing. I'll be around. And I'll see you tonight."

With a backward glance at the Wartenburg selection, Tracy moved on, determined to avoid the jumbo version of that particular toy. The points on the wheel looked a helluva lot sharper than the one Janie had used on her.

This was truly a strange new world. She hoped she was brave enough to explore it.

A flash of color caught Tracy's eye as she walked on. There — on the table in the corner — a rack of glorious fabric, silks as brilliant as jewels glowed in a rainbow of soft folds.

Drawn like a compass needle to north, she homed in on the gorgeous stuff, sighing with pleasure as she reached out to touch a piece. They were scarves, the designs betraying their oriental origin.

Tracy nearly hummed in delight. She'd always had a weakness for the pure colors used in oriental fashions and these were especially lovely. Brilliant reds and oranges melding into the yellows and sitting beside greens that would put an emerald to shame.

Carefully she unhooked one that caught her eye, finding two scarves linked into one package. She glanced at the saleswoman who was wrapping some up for another customer.

"Excuse me. These come in twos?" She held out the ones she'd chosen.

"Yep. One for each wrist. Or you can get four if you want to do the ankles as well." A pretty Oriental woman leaned over and showed Tracy the sets. Her hair was long and that wonderful silky black that so many women envied and so few possessed without the right genes.

"Okay. Thanks." Tracy stared at them, blinded for a moment at the thought of George using these scarves — to tie her down to her bed.

The black silk that had lured her featured a tiny silver dragon within its weave, barely discernible but enough to add a little sparkle to offset the glow of the soft darkness. It was incredibly light but very seductive and Tracy was helpless to resist it.

"I'll take these."

The saleswoman pulled another bag from behind her and smiled. "Good choice. I like that design too. That'll be forty-five dollars plus tax." She took Tracy's money and passed the change back. "I hope you enjoy these. They're a lot of fun."

Given what Tracy had paid for a silk scarf in town not too long ago, she considered it a bargain and was soon happily clasping a nondescript little bag containing black silk naughtiness. Exactly how she was going to explain her purchase to George, she wasn't quite sure, but she hoped the opportunity would arise.

"Thanks. I'm sure they will be."

That thought led to another and she grinned to herself as she imagined George's cock sporting a large black silk bow. He would certainly rise to the occasion, she knew.

Hmmm...

Tracy had almost reached the end of the vendor tables, passing by the one featuring an assortment of oils and liquids without stopping. Like most women, she had a pretty varied collection of creams and lotions cluttering up her bathroom cabinet. Besides, she was traveling. Those weren't the easiest things to pack discreetly or safely.

But she did linger at one last mysterious table. Prominently featured was a sort of high-tech crystal ball, the sort she'd seen at some upscale parties as a decorating accessory. One touch and the flickering mini-lightning show within would respond to fingers or lips or whatever one cared to use to touch the ball.

To her surprise, though, the ball wasn't the object for sale. A dark man stepped forward, holding a rod of some sort with a smaller glass ball on its tip. "Ever seen one of these before?"

Tracy looked up and shook her head. "No. I've seen one of *these*..." She gestured at the ball.

"Yeah. They're popular now." He nodded. "This works on the same principle." He raised the rod in his hand and Tracy noticed a thin cord coming from one end. "It's called a violet wand." He held it close to her cheek.

She jumped as a tiny crackle pinged against her skin. "Oh." She lifted a hand to touch where she'd felt the shock. "That's a good little smack you got there."

He smiled. "No harm done, I assure you. It's a loose adaptation of a Tesla coil. Gives you a small zap. Just enough to keep you awake."

"Yeah. That would keep me awake." Tracy rubbed her cheek. "Don't even ask me to think what that would feel like anyplace sensitive."

"Some people love it. They swear it brings on an orgasm that is beyond belief."

Tracy lifted one eyebrow. "And some people eat liver too."

The man laughed. "Okay. Point taken. It's interesting though, isn't it?"

"I suppose. Sorry I'm not more enthusiastic, but I think that's a guy thing, not a girl thing. Probably a guy engineer would go into raptures over it." Tracy shrugged. "Different strokes."

"Ain't that the truth?" The man gave her a friendly nod as she moved away.

Satisfied she'd checked the most interesting of the merchandise available, Tracy stepped from the barn and into the sunlight once more, her scarves tucked securely away in her purse.

She would hide them in her room, maybe under her pillow. Then tonight…oh yeah.

With a decidedly naughty grin curving her lips, Tracy headed back for the place she was coming to know quite well under a slightly different name.

Pure Sin.

* * * * *

When it came to shopping, George sucked at it. He hated to wait. Long lines and crowded shops bothered him. He usually did his grocery shopping late at night so he wouldn't be bothered. Except for the traditional walking zombies that roamed the stores at night in purple teddy bear pajamas and fuzzy bunny slippers.

George strolled into the barn and was happy to see that there weren't a lot of people around. There was a line of vendors that reminded him of a street fair, but with leather and whips instead of a thousand and one gas-inducing foods.

He passed by a table with piles of fur and figured he should keep his thoughts about shaving or not shaving pussies to himself. He smiled at the saleswoman and walked on, observing more than actually shopping. The floggers and whips display just begged for a bunch of Indiana Jones references to whip mastery. If he was going to attend a party later he didn't want to be completely stupid in the BDSM area.

Pure Sin

Most of his knowledge was from porno movies and the things he had heard from friends. This fair, these tables—well, a lot of the things he saw were very stylish and beautifully made.

He stopped walking, seeing something bright out of the corner of his eye and with a thump somebody bumped into him.

"Excuse me." A deep voice spoke behind George.

George turned to see a chest. An extremely large woman's chest, covered in black leather. He quickly stepped back and looked up. The woman was stunning. She had long flowing blonde hair and wore what resembled feminine biker gear with a mini skirt that showed off her long toned legs.

She was statuesque, to say the least of it. Her companion wasn't quite so statuesque—a light brown Chihuahua on a leash. The dog growled then barked at him. It was more of a chirp than a genuine bark, but still the dog was obviously pissed off. It was also decked out in a leather outfit complete with a spiked collar, which didn't really help its looks very much. George still regarded it as an ugly little rat.

"I'm sorry. I wasn't paying attention."

The woman placed her hand on her hip and sighed. "Next time be more careful? You almost stepped on Brutus." The woman looked down at her dog and made little sympathetic kissy noises.

You have got to be kidding me. George looked down. *Yep, definitely a rat.* The woman turned her nose up, walking away in a huff.

Turning around, George mumbled under his breath, "What a bitch."

"Oh Martin's not that bad. He's usually pretty nice to be around." A woman was straightening her display and caught George's mutterings.

"Well, she's…wait…did you say *he*? *Martin*?"

The woman smiled. "Ooops, sorry. I should've said Marty. His operation has changed him quite a bit. It's just that the hormones are making him a bit more bitchy these days."

George just shook his head and decided silence was the best way to handle the situation. The woman's booth was the one that had caught his eye so he began to examine the variety of scarves and silken things more closely. They were so colorful and glimmered in the light.

He picked up some of the fabric and rubbed it between his fingers. It was soft and smooth, similar to expensive sheets on a bed. He couldn't help but stare at how the black fabric moved like waves as it would hang and ruffle in a pile. It actually intrigued him, in a lot of ways. With a little smile he imagined Tracy wearing a nightgown or just panties made from the stuff. He swallowed. If he kept thinking like *that* he'd have to excuse himself *and* the silk scarf and find somewhere private.

The woman watched as George let the fabric drift back down to the table. "You like that?" She pointed to the scarf he had been holding.

"What? Oh it's beautiful. I'm just looking around. I guess you could say I'm a virgin here."

"There are no real virgins here, sir. If you came to our fair you are thinking about experiencing something." She gave George a once-over look and smiled. The woman was Asian with long black hair and a very elegant style to her. If George wasn't already mentally and physically locked into Tracy he would be tempted to ask this woman to dinner. There was something about her—she was very subtle and behaved in a delightfully demure fashion.

George felt the twinge of arousal through his body. "Well, my new girlfriend—or not exactly girlfriend—she's a girl—I mean a woman and a friend..." He continued to stumble for words as the woman just stared at him. Finally he stopped and threw his hands out to either side. "Okay, I've just invented a new language. Assholian."

She smiled then, a genuine grin that lit her beautifully slanted eyes. "I understand. This is a quite new thing for you. If you ever just feel like talking or have questions about us—what we do, here's my number." She reached into her silk dress pocket and handed George a small business card.

"You have a pen?" she asked.

George checked his jacket and gave her his pen.

She took the card back and scribbled something on the back of it. "That's my cell number. Just in case you want to talk this weekend."

"Thank you…" he looked at the card, "…Jin. That's a different name."

"And you are?"

"George."

She gave him a delicate little bow. "Nice to meet you, George."

"I'd better get going." George smiled back and walked down the rest of the aisle of vendors.

It was fascinating and many things were quite erotic. There were items he sure as hell wouldn't have seen had he stayed in the hotel. Some he understood, other stuff confused the hell out of him. So the afternoon wasn't a total loss even though he bumped into Marty again. Marty apologized for those hormonal mood swings and Brutus humped George's shin for three blissful minutes.

George walked back to the front door to leave. He hadn't really found anything to pick up and figured he could come back or get something later for Tracy.

"George? George?" a woman's voice called to him and he turned around.

It was Jin. She was holding a brown paper bag in her hand and walked toward him.

"Here, I wanted to give you something. Didn't want you to leave empty-handed."

"What is it?" George went to open the bag.

"No, don't open it yet. Wait until later. I'll be at the party tonight, we can talk more if you'd like." Jin took George's hand and shook it gently. "Just remember, trust. It all starts with trust."

George stood with the bag in his hand and a perplexed look on his face. He was also sporting a little bit of a hard-on that was quickly covered up by the bag Jin had given him.

He'd be back here later, back to explore a world that intrigued him, puzzled him and turned him on. And Tracy would be by his side. He couldn't figure out if that was a really good thing or a really scary thing.

As he left, he knew the hours in between would drag. He wanted to get going, get moving—start this adventure and see where it would lead. Feeling a bit like he'd done in school the day before a big exam, he sighed.

A nap. He needed a nap. He could doze away some of the afternoon, then do the shower and shave thing. Anything to kill the time before the dungeon started its official activities.

And this time, he'd be there in person—with Tracy.

Chapter Eleven

ಶಾ

Tracy gulped as they stepped over the threshold into the barn and then gasped—it was really like stepping into a nightmarish medieval fantasy or somebody's vision of hell.

"You ever hear of Dante's Inferno?" George leaned close and whispered in her ear.

"I was just thinking the same thing."

She stared around her, blinking as her eyes adjusted to the lighting. It was red, a shimmering red, highlighting leather and naked skin with an eerie glow. The walls were covered with some kind of draperies patterned in a grey stone design and combined with the red filters, the whole place seemed surreal—not in the least like what she'd seen earlier that day.

It was much bigger since the portioning curtains had been removed, opening up the entire floor space for the dungeon and its guests. The windows were covered and the sounds of people partying were more muffled than she'd expected—probably the natural result of putting fabric on the walls. Heels still clicked on the floor though, since that had been left bare of coverings.

They'd met at the door to her hotel room and walked together over to the barn. Once George had remembered his key card, of course. It seemed he might be a little nervous too since he'd forgotten it and had to dart back into his own room to get it.

But they'd managed to enter the dungeon without any problems, their keys being accepted with a smile from the leather-and-studded girl manning the registration table next to the door.

Both of them slowed their pace then stopped, stunned by the room before them, trying to take it all in.

There was music playing somewhere, a steady drumbeat beneath the other sounds. Those other sounds—Tracy realized it was the slap of something against something else, punctuated by little cries and whimpers. And there was the steady buzz of conversation too.

As her eyes focused, she found they were standing near a strange contraption, a bar suspended from one of the beams crisscrossing the old ceiling. And from the bar something else was suspended.

A man.

Naked but for a black leather vest, his arms were stretched taut above him and he stood, legs apart and head lowered, tethered securely to his restraints. Behind him a woman strode backward and forward, her sharp stilettos clattering a little on the stone floor. She held a flogger in her hand and when the spirit moved her she lashed out at the man's ass, making him jerk and shudder.

Tracy jerked and shuddered too. It was so—unexpected. She watched open-mouthed as the man writhed and whimpered but didn't protest. And she couldn't help noticing he had one helluva hard-on going for himself, erect as could be and thrusting from a clean-shaven groin.

The woman lashed him again, calmly taking her time about it. Besides the high heels, she wore a leather outfit that clung to her generous curves. Almost. The high-cut legs nearly revealed whether she'd shaved more than her bikini line and her breasts were rippling like waves about to break over the top of the corset. She was blonde, stacked and pretty damn lethal too.

"*Holy shit.*"

Obviously George had noticed her. Or he was sympathizing with the guy getting his ass whupped. Either way it was pretty damn intense. "I'd hate to meet that woman in a dark room after pissing her off."

Before Tracy had a chance to say anything, a petite blonde woman appeared in front of her. "Hi. Are you Tracy?"

"Yes." A light clicked on in her brain. "You're Amy, aren't you? Mike's girlfriend?"

"That's me." She smiled at George. "Mike said you'd both be here tonight and I was to look out for you."

"Uh, what? Oh that's nice of him." George cleared his throat and looked Amy right in the eye. Which kept his gaze off the bare breasts that weren't quite covered by her soft leather vest.

Amy giggled. "Always glad to help out new friends." She waved a hand at herself. "Sorry about the lack of clothing. I usually wear more than this to a dungeon, but I just had my nipples pierced. Can't stand much of anything rubbing against 'em."

Tracy cringed. "Oh wow. Yeah. I can believe that." She was vaguely aware of a stirring in her own nipples, a sensation that they were retreating somewhere safe — like Tasmania.

"You wanna see?" Amy reached for the tie on her vest.

"*No no.* Really. Thanks." Tracy almost stuttered. She really did not want to see anybody's nipples, pierced or not.

George's smile quickly changed to a frown. "Maybe later." He mumbled.

"Okay." Amy smiled sunnily. "Let's go look around, shall we?"

Tracy felt the odd urge to grip George's hand as they moved farther into the dungeon. Falling down a rabbit hole couldn't be much stranger than *this*. Tracy felt a real empathy for Alice.

Coming toward them was a tall man, soberly dressed in black from head to foot. No studs or leather for him, just a nice—and probably very expensive—silk T-shirt and impeccable black pants.

"Oh good. Here's a guy you both should meet." Amy stopped and waited as he approached them. "Hi, Master Damien."

He nodded at Amy. "Good to see you, Amy. Are these Mike's friends?"

"Yep. Tracy and George." Amy glanced over her shoulder. "This is Master Damien. He's the power behind this whole dungeon. Puts it all together for us, keeps us from getting into too much trouble…" She giggled.

Master Damien lifted an eyebrow. "Something I've totally failed with you, young lady." The grin took any sting out of his words. "Nice to meet you, George. Tracy." He shook hands with George and nodded at Tracy.

Another Dominant. Tracy wasn't sure how she knew, but there was something very assured about his manner, a cool confidence that she sensed deep within him. When he looked at her—she felt she was being assessed, her good points cataloged and probably her faults as well.

She had the oddest urge to curtsey. *Sheesh.* He was *damn* good.

He had to be the other side of fifty and perhaps it was his age, coupled with his experience, that gave him that "air". Whatever it was, Tracy could well believe he was the man behind it all. He just reeked of control and efficiency. If he owned a company, she'd bet her last dollar it was right up there in the Fortune 500 listings.

Greetings concluded, Master Damien laid a hand on George's shoulder. "Walk with me, George. I'd be delighted to show you around. This place can be a little overwhelming the first time you see it."

George glanced at Tracy. "Well, sure. Okay. That would be great."

Tracy hesitated. "I don't want us to keep you from anything important, M-Master Damien—" She stuttered a little as she spoke his name. She wasn't used to addressing anybody by that title and wasn't even sure if she should be speaking to him. Perhaps she should be on her knees or something.

God*damn*. There was so much she didn't know.

"Don't worry. Amy will take good care of you, Tracy. Just for a little while. I'll return George to you in one piece." He smiled—real humor lighting his dark eyes.

"So I'll see you in a bit. If I get lost, send a search party." George lifted his shoulders and let them fall. They were both out of their element here. When in a dungeon, do as the dungeoneers do.

"C'mon, Tracy. I want to check out Janice and Jim." Amy linked her arm through Tracy's and led her away from George and Master Damien.

* * * * *

George knew his eyes were probably bugging out of his head as he feverishly tried to take in everything around him. It was…ominous to say the least. For every leather-clad person he saw, there would also be someone almost nude. The abundance of breasts damn near blinded him and made his heart want to sing the praises of ripe flesh.

"How you doing, George?" Damien took a drink from his water bottle, waiting for a response. "George?"

"Whaaa? Sorry, I was a bit distracted. Did you say something?" He looked at Damien and took a deep breath to clear his head. "Damn, there is a *lot* of crazy odd shit here."

"I'm sure it does seem odd to you at first. When you've seen as many as I have, however…"

George pointed and realized his hand was shaking. "That guy? He's got clothes-pins on his *nut sack*!" He grimaced as he spoke the words and lowered his hands instinctively to the front of his pants.

"Some people find that appealing. The pain heightens their sensations. It's not for everybody though." Damien took another drink of water and put his hand on George's shoulder to lead him down the aisle farther. "If you need something cool, we have a table with water and soft drinks on it. It's important to keep hydrated in a dungeon."

"I'm good right now, thanks." *Although if I keep sweating, I'm gonna need a gallon or two later on.*

As they walked, Damien kept up a commentary describing the various toys and activities they passed. "Have you ever used a flogger?"

"No. Not sure I could whip some woman on the ass with something like that. I'm okay with a nice hand slap or two during sex but…" George stopped talking as he and Damien reached one wall where a high table and a few barstools were arranged. There were some empty soda cans off to one side. George guessed it was for anybody who wanted a break, someplace to sit for a few minutes between punishments. If they could sit at all, that was.

There were three people there, two women and a man, and as George watched, the man leaned back into one of the women standing behind his barstool.

"You see the little woman with black hair?" Damien's voice was quiet.

"Damien. Those are *twins*."

"I know, but you see the one to the left?"

"Twins—semi *naked* twins."

Damien chuckled. "Enjoying this, are you?"

"A perfect pair. *Twins*. Have I died and gone to heaven?" George was almost drooling as he stared at the two women caressing and teasing the man, who was very muscular and tanned. Even though one was blonde and the other had long black hair, their faces and bodies were identical. They wore nothing but simple black leather thongs and stiletto-heeled boots. They were unquestionably twins—very shapely twins—one of George's darkest fantasies.

The two men stood watching as the black-haired one teased her man. The other woman seemed to be more sensual and stroked the man's neck and chest. Her red lips traced his ears and pulled gently on the lobes as she rubbed her breasts against his back. It was certainly affecting the man because the snug fit of his black jeans showed the outline of his aroused cock.

The black-haired twin noticed and stroked the bulge through his pants. Her playful actions seemed to stir and perhaps upset the man, but she kept doing it even after he'd pull her hands away from where she toyed with him.

"This is…kinda cool. What's this all about?"

"Just watch, George. I know these girls. The guy is their Dom. He has a beautiful bike too. A Harley I think. Never mind…just watch."

The black-haired woman began to kiss the man's chest as the blonde woman continued whispering and caressing his neck and shoulders with her erect nipples rubbing against his sweaty back. The man jerked himself free of them, stood up rigidly and glared at the black-haired woman after she bit his nipple. The blonde pulled him back into her nude body.

"*Fuck*, you bitch."

She bit him once more, in spite of his obvious anger, then wrinkled her nose cheekily and giggled.

The man's chest rose and fell with deep breaths as the woman dragged her nails through the thin hair then glanced up at him, leaned forward, bared her teeth and raked them over his skin. The guy quickly grabbed the girl and held her by the arms.

George noticed that nobody else watching moved as the guy easily manhandled the smaller woman. He bent her over a stool and reached for the shelf. He picked up a red-handled flogger with black strands of leather hanging from it.

The sound of the flogger against the woman's bare flesh echoed in George's head. It wasn't a cracking like a whip as much as the sound of a slap. A loud, painful slap. Growing up, George remembered the spanking he'd gotten from his father's belt for stealing something. He'd never forgotten that sound—and this was the same. He tried not to cringe but knew it must hurt this little woman.

George watched her face, expecting to see the agonized reaction in her eyes. Each time the man swung his arm back then let another blow fall on her ass, a euphoric glaze crossed the woman's pale face. Her body would jolt forward with each strike but a blissful glow rose to the surface of her skin.

The woman wasn't just *enjoying* this—she got off on it.

George looked at the man's reactions as well as the woman's. His eyes were opened wide and crinkled a little as he smiled. The sweat beaded on his forehead and his body shone with heat. With one last swing he struck the woman's ass hard and loudly.

Her eyelids fluttered and a few tears trickled down her cheeks. She sighed, holding back what had to be some pretty strong emotions from the pain. As the man breathed hard and deep the black haired woman moved over to him and rested her head against his shoulder. The blonde woman got up and stroked her twin's naked spine. All three held each other tightly.

George was confused as he and Damien walked away. "What the fuck was that? The guy whips her ass hard enough to leave welts and she curls up like a puppy next to him?"

"She asked for it, George. She *wanted* it. Things aren't as cookie-cutter basic as you might think here. Everybody has different needs. That girl was what we call a *brat*. The other one, her twin, was part of the game they play. Trust me—she'll get hers with their Dom later. And when they get that guy alone somewhere, he'll get his too."

"Different strokes, I guess." George shrugged and they turned to look around some more. "A good portion of this—well, it's not so much about the sex, is it?"

Damien shook his head. "No. And I'm glad you're beginning to realize that. Sure there's nudity and yes, a lot of these games are sexual in nature. You put a naked man together with a naked woman and most of the time they're going to think sex."

George's eyes drifted over a tall woman leading a handsome younger man behind her by a chain linking his wrists. Both were nearly nude. "Um, yeah."

"But this is much *more* about trust." Damien touched him on the shoulder. "Trust and the surrendering of control, one partner to another. Some just let it happen in the bedroom. Most people do, actually. There are others for whom it's a lifestyle choice. They live it twenty-four seven."

"Really?"

"Sure. It's a struggle. That kind of existence requires a massive commitment on both parts. A lifetime commitment as a matter of fact. I know. I've trained some of them." He grinned. "Don't even think about that yet. Just find out if it's something you and your lady might enjoy. Take your time. Explore what gives you pleasure and what gives her pleasure. You'll find they're one and the same."

George considered the idea. "So even though I'm in control and…and…doing what I want to do, she's going to be enjoying it?"

"Unless you tie her to the bed and then go off to watch the first seven innings of a baseball game, sure." Damien chuckled.

"Now there's an idea. I wonder if it would work during the playoffs…hmmm." George rubbed his chin.

"George, you will be in control of this woman. She will obey your every command. In return, she will be getting just about one hundred percent of your attention. For as long as you choose. She will have no choice but to do what you tell her. She will lie down, turn over, suck you, fuck you, please you in any way you wish. And all the time you will be *totally focused on her*. It's an exchange of gifts, really. To have her satisfying you, coming when you allow it—is a source of mutual pleasure for you both."

Something inside George stirred as he considered Master Damien's words. To have a woman completely surrender…completely at his command…*sheeeit*!

"One thing though." Damien paused. "You ever hear of SSC?"

George thought for a moment. "Don't think so. Spit and Swallow Club?"

"No." Damien chuckled. "It means Safe, Sane and Consensual. An absolute rule. No matter what you see here tonight, George, it's always safe, sane and between consensual parties. Never doubt that, no matter how outrageous it may look."

"Makes a lot of sense." George was thoughtful. Then other thoughts intruded. "Um…is there a restroom in this place?"

"Sure. Over there in the corner, you'll see a door. Just go through. Second on the left."

"Thanks. I'll be right back."

* * * * *

After freeing his monster, George let out a huge sigh. He rested his hand on the ceramic tile wall and closed his eyes, enjoying his well-earned relief. There were only a few other things as refreshing as a good pee after holding it for thirty minutes. He should have gone before he left, but he was too damn nervous to think about it.

Whew, I needed this. His moment of relief was interrupted as a loud thud followed by a whoosh of air disturbed the silence.

"Fuck, I need to piss so bad my back teeth are floating. Dammit, ooooh shit, I'm not going to make it." The man's voice seemed desperate.

George scooted a bit closer in typical male fashion, doing his best to modestly hide the package. *Call it ego, call it fear, call it whatever – but it's the way of the male animal across the land.* He just looked down and silently talked to his partner in crime, who stared expressionlessly back at him.

With gaze lowered, he couldn't help but notice as a pair of black pointy high-heeled shoes swam into his line of sight. A slow glance upward had him peeking at a leather skirt wrapped around some shapely legs. Something about those legs seemed familiar.

"I know you." A voice sounded loud above his right ear.

Oh shit! He looked up and saw long blonde hair pulled back and a wicked smile. "Uh hello." George shook and tucked away his monster then tugged the handle to flush the urinal.

"Remember me? I'm Marty. Fancy seeing *you* in here." She finished up her own activities, flushed then turned to face George.

"George—my name is George." He rinsed his hands in the small sink then used a paper towel to dry them. Fighting not to look anyplace else, just in case, George focused on Marty's eyes reflected in the mirror above the sink.

And totally failed to keep his gaze where it ought to be. As Marty looked down to straighten her clothing, so did George. It was bad enough that Marty was going through a sex change and was already an attractive-looking woman, now George had the image of a definitely male cock stuck in his mind. And it wasn't a pretty image, either. Marty was rather well endowed, lifestyle choices and hormones notwithstanding.

Marty looked up and noticed George peeking. "Pretty soon I won't have to walk around with this thing anymore.

They're going to take it off and give me a nice little pussy to go with this perfect set of breasts." She tucked her cock into a leather pocket cleverly strapped along her inner thigh. After finishing, Marty pulled a bit on the leather skirt and George was impressed—he couldn't tell Marty was packing anything at all, let alone a respectably sized cock.

"I wish I had a little pussy myself, but that's—never mind." George stopped himself short of asking the question that danced on the tip of his tongue.

"Typical." Marty checked himself—or herself—in the mirror. "You try growing up not knowing why you've got all the equipment a man has, but knowing you're not supposed to have it. That you're really supposed to be a woman."

George just had to continue his thought. "If you don't mind, I just gotta ask. Why? Why get everything changed? Call me stupid but this has always been something that I understand to a point then just don't *get*. Can't you just stay like you are? You've got everything a woman would envy—you can wear clothes that make you look like a gorgeous showgirl..."

"Would you fuck me, George?"

"Pardon?"

"If you didn't know what you know about me and we'd just met, like over drinks or something, would you fuck me?"

After a few seconds of pondering, George answered. Tall, long legs, blonde hair, great tits, tight body—his first reaction, since he knew the truth, had him swallowing back a gag in his throat. But he needed to be honest. "Probably. If I didn't know and saw you somewhere? I'd be inclined to talk to you and—whatever."

"Okay. Thanks for that. It's a nice compliment. Let's go a step further. If you and I went to bed and I bent over, would you fuck me in the ass?"

Confused, George stuttered "What—um—what are you getting at?"

"I'm asking to help you understand something. No kinky come-ons here, I swear. Just answer the question."

"I guess so. If you asked me to."

Marty nodded, an odd expression on her face. "Well, how would you feel if you were fucking what you *think* is a woman and a pair of hairy balls are slapping against *your* balls as you fuck?"

George blinked then winced as a tiny shiver danced over every inch of his skin, landing with a crash into his brain cells.

"Thanks for the second visual I will never be able to wipe from my memory." He gulped. "I get your point. You want to be a woman in as many ways as possible."

Marty smiled. "Now you're catching on."

George lifted his hands and spread them wide in a gesture of confusion. "You know, these last couple of days— I've gotten pummeled by a shitload of stuff I don't know how to understand. I'm sorry if I made you uncomfortable."

Marty shook head and grinned. "You didn't. I know who's genuinely interested and who's just looking for an excuse to razz on me." He glanced into the mirror and ran a finger under his eye. "Damn mascara is smudging."

George couldn't help a little chuckle at the purely feminine gesture.

Marty turned back to him. "You know something? I've been coming to these things for a few years now. Both early on before I got comfortable with this…" He waved his hands at his body. "And later when I became what I wanted to be. This dungeon is a place where I can be free to be myself. The person I really am."

He glanced back into the mirror over the sink. "I like who I am." His gaze met George's. "Same applies to you, George. You can be anything you want to be. A dominant, a sub, it doesn't matter. Nobody judges you." He rinsed his hands and continued. "I can be the woman I want to be and it's so refreshing to *not* be worried what others think. Fuck the people who don't understand, and who look down on me, or think I'm a pervert. I don't care what they think. It's nice to know there aren't any of those people here. Just have fun, George. Take from the dungeon what you want—it's an eye-opening experience." He tossed the paper towel in the trash after drying his hands. "Don't judge, don't assume and don't let your inhibitions get in the way."

"Thanks, Marty." George absorbed Marty's words and his advice.

They stood in the men's room like two guys during halftime at a football game as the door swung open. A grey-haired man nodded at them and headed toward the urinals.

"I gotta run." Marty walked toward George, grabbed his face in his large hands and planted a kiss right on George's lips. Then he left, leaving George speechless.

"That's one fine-looking woman you've got there." The gray-haired man made the comment as he flushed the urinal.

George hurried to the sink, filling his hand with water and washing out his mouth as best he could. He did it several times then swallowed a couple of mouthfuls of the cool liquid. "That fucker slipped me the tongue."

"Lucky guy." The old man, who'd waited patiently behind George, washed and dried his hands and the two of them walked out.

"Er...George? Do you know you're wearing lipstick?" Damien raised an eyebrow in question as George rejoined him in the dungeon.

"Shit. I am? Well, I must've got it when Marty kissed me." He grabbed a napkin and rubbed his mouth.

"Marty?"

"Yeah, in the men's room."

"I don't know if I should ask." Damien was clearly fighting the urge to laugh.

"Please don't. It's bad enough I had to see his big dick. Then he kissed me and shoved his tongue into my mouth."

"Okay." Damien schooled his features into a calm expression, leaving only an unsettling hint of a smile around his eyes. "I think at this point we need to see if we can get you a breath mint."

George couldn't agree more.

"Damien? You old Dom bastard, how are you doing?"

George turned at the sound of a voice calling to Damien, his attention caught by a beautiful brunette wearing not much more than a black collar and leash. His gaze followed the leash to see a man holding the other end, talking to Damien. A midget, holding a leash on a stunning, black-vinyl micro-mini dressed woman twice his size.

There's something you don't see every day.

Damien bent down and laughed as he talked to the little guy. George stood quietly, trying his best not to stare at the erect nipples poking out of the cutouts in the tight vinyl outfit the woman wore.

"So…have you been to a dungeon like this before?" Perhaps a little small talk would be nice. She didn't answer, just smiled a little then lowered her gaze, looking down at the guy holding her leash.

"I'm George, by the way." He held out his hand automatically.

"Hey, what the fuck are you doing?" The little man looked up crossly at George.

"Me? Nothing. I was just being polite."

"If you want to talk to her you ask *me*, motherfucker."

George didn't know what to say or what he'd do if the guy went after him. The last thing he'd want was to have this guy take a swing at him when his nuts were at perfect height for the guy to do some major damage.

Damien rested a hand on the shorter man's shoulder. "Rick, he's new here. He doesn't understand our rules yet. This is George."

"Okay, sorry." Rick relaxed. "I come to these things all the time and every now and again some asshole tries to fuck with me and Sherri."

"That's because they don't know about how you got your nickname—*Rick-The-Dick*."

The girl giggled and Rick smiled at her then tugged her leash to lower her head so that he could give her a kiss. "Go ahead. You can talk to him, Sherri."

George reached down to shake Rick's hand and then nodded toward Sherri politely. "I'm sorry, Rick. This whole scene is new to me. I'm here with a woman I met recently. We want to know about all this and…well, I guess you could say we were real interested."

"No problem. Damien is probably the best guy to steer you right. Of course if you want a woman's opinion…I'd say you couldn't do better than talk to Jin. That woman is so fine. If it wasn't for me being married and so in love with my Sherri…I tell you, buddy." Rick raised his eyebrows and licked his lips as he grinned wickedly.

"Jin? I met her earlier, I think." George paused. "Very nice woman. That long black hair and that slim body and…" He stopped, noticing that the three of them seemed to be nodding their heads in time with each other.

Apparently, his appreciation of Jin and her assets was something they all shared. Then he glimpsed a familiar head across the dungeon.

Tracy.

George's attention immediately drifted away from Jin, Master Damien, Rick and Sherri. He licked his lips, hoping all traces of Marty's lipstick were gone. He sure as hell didn't want to have to explain that to Tracy. There were other things he wanted to explain, other matters he wanted to discuss with her.

And these matters involved the two of them—naked. A bolt of lust hardened his cock at the mere thought.

He wanted Tracy. *Now.*

Chapter Twelve

Amy had firmly steered Tracy away from George and Master Damien, strolling along one side of the room, smiling and waving hello as she did so.

"Wow. You know everybody, huh?" Tracy couldn't help the comment.

"Sure. We're regulars, mostly. This has been an ongoing thing now for a couple of years."

They neared a section of the wall where a woman was tied up and spread-eagled on a tall wooden contraption shaped like an X. Tracy's steps slowed. "What's that?"

Amy glanced over. "That's a St. Andrew's Cross."

"The position?"

"No, the thing she's on." Amy stopped. "It's a very common piece of equipment in dungeons like this. For obvious reasons."

The woman wore nothing but a fishnet body suit, split open at the crotch, and her body was splayed helplessly, breasts thrusting forward and pussy opened to anybody who cared to look. Tracy watched as two other women began caressing her, teasing her a little, slapping her gently beside her breasts and tugging at her nipples.

Then a man stepped forward and the two women immediately backed away, lowering their eyes to the floor.

"Are they...*submissives*?"

Amy grinned. "Yes. All three of them. Charlie is their Dominant. Watch his technique."

Tracy watched, feeling a little like a Peeping Tom. But others had paused as well. She and Amy weren't the only ones observing this performance—if that was the right word.

Charlie pulled something sparkling from one pocket and began working on his sub's nipples, extending them and slipping the glittering things over them. A chain linked the two and when he was satisfied with the positioning, he tugged it.

Tracy felt her mouth drop as a whimper of sound came from the bound woman's throat.

"Ouch." Tracy didn't even realize she'd said the word aloud. She leaned to Amy. "Doesn't that hurt?"

"Sort of. At first anyway. But then it's nothing but a pleasure. Every touch on the chain, every movement—it makes your clit ache. Really arousing, lemme tell ya."

Filing that information away, Tracy kept her eyes on the group around the cross. At a sign from Charlie, the other two women had returned and were now delicately running their tongues over the distended nipples, allowing Charlie plenty of room to continue his activities.

Tracy felt her eyebrows rise as he knelt before his submissive and began to tug at her pussy lips. Once again a piece of jewelry appeared and was fastened to the woman, although whether he'd actually clipped it to her clit or her labia, Tracy couldn't tell. And she wasn't about to go any nearer to find out.

"Isn't that beautiful?" Amy stared too. "See how each part of her shines for her Master?"

Tracy nodded. "Yes." Her thoughts were pretty scattered at this point, so she kept her answer simple.

Then Charlie produced a short whip. The women stepped back once more with a last lingering caress and Charlie began to demonstrate his "technique". Several short quick lashes followed, on hips and belly and thighs.

"He starts with the well-padded areas. See?" Amy's voice was quite clinical although a little hushed. She could have been an announcer at a golf tournament. *And now Charlie is going to go for par — a difficult nine-iron shot over the hip bone and onto the ass cheeks — let's watch...*

Trying to pull her head out of its descent into irrelevant insanity, Tracy kept her gaze fixed on the strange tableau. Charlie's movements were becoming rhythmic; a firm swing to one side then the other, striking his submissive carefully yet more strongly as he found his pace.

The jewels glittered as the woman began to writhe, hips thrusting forward, head lolling back as she moaned slightly.

He left few marks on her body, probably no more than the straining fishnet would leave when she took off her bodysuit. But when he neared her breasts and alternated them with her pussy, she began to cry out and shudder.

"Yes, oh God, Master — *please*. Yessss..."

He stopped immediately. "Not yet. When I say so."

Her head fell forward, her eyes downcast. "Yes, Master. When you say so."

Tracy gulped and turned to Amy. "How long will he keep this up?"

Amy shrugged. "Until he's ready." She looked away. "Oh I see Jim's warming up. Want to move on? They could be a while here..."

Tracy turned away from the cross and the party of four. "Sure." She followed Amy to one corner of the room where a naked woman lay on her back atop a large trestle table.

Behind her was a very tall man with a completely shaved head. "Hi, Amy."

"Hey, Jim. I'm so glad you could make it." Amy did her friendly thing. "Hey, Janice. How ya doin', girl?"

The girl on the table waved. "Doin' good, babe. How's that dishy boyfriend of yours?"

"Working tonight. He's going to be real sorry he missed you guys." She turned a little. "This is Tracy. It's her first dungeon. Can we watch a bit?"

Jim smiled at Tracy. "Welcome, honey. Sure you can watch."

"Thanks. Nice to meet you—both." Tracy was out of her depth. What the hell did one say to a naked woman lying on a table? She made an effort to push her inhibitions way down to the back of her brain. Nobody cared about nudity, apparently. Nobody cared about cellulite or weight issues or diet plans.

They were *themselves*, period. It was—oddly refreshing. Tracy knew her perceptions were shifting a little the longer she stayed. This wasn't about how people *looked*, it was about who they *were*. Janice was no skinny supermodel. She was a well-built woman whose full breasts comfortably sagged to either side of her chest. Her belly was rounded, her thighs would never be found on the pages of a lingerie catalog.

She was *real*. Her skin was creamy white and it suddenly struck Tracy that there wasn't a hair in sight. No nubby traces of a recent shaving either. This was a woman who'd had a hellaciously fine wax job.

Within moments she discovered why.

Jim had been busying himself with what looked like a massive swab—a cotton ball soaked in something or other. He swiped it over one of Janice's nipples. "Ready, sweetheart?"

Janice grinned. "Oh yeah."

Tracy gasped aloud as Jim lit the swab and brushed it once more over Janice, leaving a blue flame burning over her skin. Within seconds he smoothed his hand through the fire, totally extinguishing it.

"Oh *wow*!" This time it was Tracy who was totally absorbed.

"Yeah. Fire play. Isn't it neat?"

Amy's words bounced off Tracy. She was completely fascinated. "Janice, I have to ask—does it burn? Can you feel anything?"

"Not a thing." Janice turned her head. "Just a sort of cool warmth—it's hard to explain."

"Tracy?" Jim spoke from behind Janice. "Hold out your hand."

Tracy did so without hesitation, palm upward, extending her arm over Janice's breasts toward Jim. He repeated his earlier movements, swiping the cotton ball over her palm then igniting it.

Seconds later he gently caressed her hand and extinguished the flames, but for those few moments...

"Oh my God. *I held fire!*" She looked at Jim. "I really did. I held it. Right here in my hand..."

"Didn't hurt, did it?" Janice chuckled.

"No." Tracy stared at her palm. "No. It's the wildest thing..." She looked back at Jim. "Thanks—that was incredible."

"You're welcome."

"Jim's the best at this." Amy was observing the whole thing with interest. "Although he's gonna have to stop doing it any minute now and go back to his regular wax play."

"He is?"

"Yeah. We're not really licensed for fire. Gotta watch those regulations." Amy tipped her head warningly over her shoulder. "Master Damien's here, Jim."

Tracy looked around too. And there he was, on the other side of the barn with George. Guiltily, Tracy realized that for a while she'd almost forgotten about them. It was so—so—surreal, that her mind had simply refused to focus on anything other than what was in front of her.

She did, however, notice a striking Oriental woman standing next to George and smiling up at him. They were talking, gesturing about something and the woman rested her hand on George's arm for a moment as he smiled down at her.

She thought the woman might have been the one selling those silk scarves at the fair earlier, but at this distance and in the low light, it was hard to tell. All she could really see was about a mile of silky black hair and something red and shiny hugging the woman's body. Tracy felt a sharp pang of what might well have been jealousy.

Hmm. What was *that* about?

As they said goodbye to Jim and Janice, it all crashed back into Tracy. She was here because she intended to surrender to George. To become his sexual submissive. But she sure as hell wasn't going to go buy a St. Andrew's Cross. So what *was* she going to do?

"Amy?" They paused by a table with soft drinks on it. "Can I ask you something?"

"Sure, Tracy. Anything. That's what I'm here for."

"Is that a turn-on? The fire thing?" Tracy looked around. "How much of this is about getting…aroused? Sexually?"

Amy thought for a moment. "Some of it is, some isn't. I don't know about the fire. Maybe on the breasts or the pussy? Could be." She thought some more. "Tracy, this is about doing what feels good. Or bad. There is a very strong sexual component to most of this play. But there are many people here who've gone past that simple element and into areas of domination and submission that you and I can only guess at. Their needs and their motivations are different than ours."

Tracy let her eyes wander around, trying to take it all in. Trying to *understand*…

"I'm a submissive. Mike's my Dom. But it only goes as far as the bedroom door. I wouldn't walk through the supermarket with a collar and a leash. But if Mike wants me to wear one in bed…sure. I'll wear one. Knowing I'm turning him on turns me on too."

"I guess that makes sense…" Tracy knew her tone wasn't exactly confident.

"Look." Amy offered her a soda and Tracy gladly accepted it, grabbing onto it like it was a life preserver and she was drowning. "Sex is different things for different people. For most folks, it's a fifty-fifty deal these days, right? Each partner brings something to bed with them. But that also means that if one partner doesn't make it, they worry they did something wrong."

She sighed. "I'm not explaining this very well."

"No, really, go on. Anything you tell me will help at this point."

"'Kay." Amy sipped her soda. "So when you submit to your man, the numbers change. It becomes ninety percent *him*. He gets to call the shots, to have you do what will give him the most pleasure."

"Okay." Tracy nodded.

"The kicker is that what gives *him* the most pleasure relieves *you* of having to think about that. You know he's going to enjoy this. He's going to make sure of it. So all you have to worry about is doing what he says and then reaping the rewards. Because sure as shit he's going to make *you* happy at the same time. When you free your mind of any concerns about his pleasure you can focus on your own."

Tracy thought about that. "It sort of makes sense."

Amy smiled. "It'll make more sense once you've done it."

"But…" So many questions, so many things raced through Tracy's head. "What about the whippings? The fire? All that stuff?"

Amy waved them away. "All toys, trappings of play, doll. Some folks like the sting of a flogger on their ass. Others like to spank and be spanked." She paused, thinking. "I guess it's like some folks who get a kick out of lotions or vibrators—or silk sheets. Everybody's tastes are a little different. Here we go for more clearly defined roles—dominant and submissive. But it's

Pure Sin

all consensual, fulfilling needs that we have. Just not the same way that others do."

She crumpled her can. "You hear of the SSC rule?"

Tracy shook her head. "What's that?"

"Safe, Sane and Consensual. An *absolute* rule. Everything that takes place in a BDSM environment or between BDSM partners has to meet those requirements. All the activities you see around you, whether gentle or extreme, they're all safe, sane and consensual. It's a must. No way do we *ever* break it."

"Like the safe word?" Tracy remembered that from someplace.

"Exactly." Amy nodded. "You'll see. Once you give the gift of your submission to George and let him take control—all things become possible. And you will never want to go back. Trust me on this. It can lead to orgasms beyond anything you can imagine. And it's empowering too."

Tracy felt the color rise in her cheeks. "It is, huh?"

"You betcha." Amy chuckled. "Because even though you're submitting to your partner, *you're* the one with the ultimate control. One word and it stops. Just knowing that, well, it's damn near addictive. Makes me hot just thinking about it." She winced. "Not a good idea with newly pierced nipples either."

"Oh *Jesus*." Tracy couldn't help smiling. Amy was nothing if not open when it came to sharing personal information.

"How about we go find that man of yours?"

Tracy tossed her soda can into the recycling bin and took a deep breath. "Okay."

* * * * *

They moved toward each other somewhat awkwardly, Tracy almost hesitant to look at George. Would he be any different? Had he changed his mind? What did he think about everything that was going on around them?

She couldn't tell. He simply stopped and waited for her to join him and Master Damien.

"Hey." She cleared her throat and tried again. "Interesting, huh?"

He nodded, face expressionless for the moment. "Yeah. Really interesting."

"Amy…" Master Damien spoke quietly. "I think we need to stop by and chat with Jim. I understand he's going to be doing his *wax play*…" The words were emphasized and Tracy hid a grin as Amy nodded respectfully. "Sure thing, Master Damien. I always enjoy watching Jim."

They left together, Amy giving Tracy a quick wink over her shoulder. She really was a delightful girl, full of life and joy. And on another level, Tracy kind of hated to see her leave.

Swallowing, she turned back to George. "So. Um…you have a good time with the Master?"

George nodded. "Yeah. He's a real interesting guy. It was…educational, to say the least. How about you and Amy?"

Tracy nodded too. "Educational sort of covers it, yes."

Silence fell between them. Then George chuckled and reached for her hand. "Bit overwhelming, isn't it?"

She sagged against his shoulder. "No kidding."

They strolled together, hand in hand, quietly passing the various activities that were now building in intensity.

Tracy paused next to a couple who were obviously serious adherents to the BDSM lifestyle. The woman was kneeling, hands bound behind her, a ball-gag in her mouth and her naked ass pushing high into the air as she bent over a low bench. The leather corset was laced very tightly, making her flesh bulge beneath the stays.

Her Dom was behind her, giving her a thorough punishment with a cane. The marks on her buttocks were red and angry, though obviously administered with some sort of restraint. It was a criss-cross of marks, symmetrically growing to cover her white skin.

Tracy's fingers tightened around George's hand. "I will say, here and now, that if you ever think to do something like *that* to me," she nodded at the couple, "I will break every bone in your body."

George nodded and moved her up to the next bench. This time a man was submitting, also bound, but stark naked this time. His desired punishment was a line of wooden clothes pegs artistically arranged along the soft skin of his balls. With his knees spread wide, they were clearly visible, as was the sweat dotting his spine. George had seen him earlier but still flinched and wanted to cross his legs to protect his family jewels at the sight.

"Likewise." It was more of a croak than a word, but Tracy got the message loud and clear as a shudder passed through George. "Fuck, shit, damn."

Tracy tugged his hand. "So no pain, okay?"

"No pain. It doesn't do it for me. I don't find that…appealing or arousing." George glanced around. "Although I guess some folks do." He looked back at Tracy. "Has this changed your mind?"

She stared steadily back at him. "I don't think so. Has it changed yours?"

"Nope." He met her gaze. Then grinned. "I still have that fantasy about twins."

"Twins, huh?" She shook her head.

Men. All this crazy stuff going on, a night ahead that promised whole bunches more fun and all he could talk about was frickin' twins.

They must have been there for quite some time, since the noise level had increased considerably. Used to the sound of leather on flesh, Tracy found she could almost ignore it, but the one thing she couldn't ignore was the panting and rhythmic cries of a woman not too far away.

George heard it too and they both turned to see what was going on.

Tracy gulped as they reached the source of the noise. Talk about a party in *full swing*...

A woman was bound into some kind of leather device suspended from an arch of metal poles. Her wrists were pulled to either side, her ass barely resting on a small leather seat and her thighs and ankles pulled wide apart, also held by black leather—wide stripes that stood out clearly against her pale skin.

Between her legs stood a man, naked but for black leather chaps. He was swinging her, pushing her on and off his cock, making her whimper out those cries Tracy had heard so clearly.

She was utterly helpless and to judge from her expression, enjoying every damn minute of it.

"Wow." George stared at the couple. "Jeez, that's *cool*..."

"Yeah. They are nice chaps, aren't they?"

"I didn't mean...I was talking about *that* contraption..." George's gaze remained fixed on the sensual swing. "Wonder what kind of support beams you'd need to hold one of those..."

Tracy rolled her eyes. For her part, she didn't care about the engineering side of things. The simple fucking part was turning her on. Of all the things she'd seen tonight, the nudity, the unashamed display of cocks and shaved pussies—it was something this simple that was finally getting *her* pussy wet.

"Oh...oh..." The woman's head fell back and her mouth opened wide on a shriek, only to turn to a groan as her partner's hands grasped her and stopped her mid-swing.

"Shit, *shit,* Mark—please—" Frantically her arms twisted in the leather straps and Tracy could see the woman's thighs shaking. She was *almost* there, and that bastard had stopped millimeters short of heaven. "You motherfucking *asshole*…finish me or I swear I'll rip your cock off and use it to stir my next martini."

Mark was grinning, even as his ass muscles flexed hard, keeping his body buried in hers. "You will, huh?"

George's hand clenched convulsively around Tracy's and she glanced up at him. "Getting to you too?"

"She's so fucking *close*…I can almost feel it…"

"Yeah. But he's in *control* of her, George. Her body, her climax—everything. She isn't going to get there until he allows her to."

George blinked and turned to Tracy. "It's what all this is about, isn't it? The giving and taking control?"

She nodded, watching his face.

"Would you…" He paused a second or two. "Is that…um…good for a woman?"

Tracy kept her eyes on his. "Yes."

George turned away just as Mark began to move once more. "Okay then." He dragged air into his lungs. "*Okay*."

* * * * *

They walked back to the inn, still hand in hand but silent now, each busy with their thoughts. There was a hell of a lot to think about too. George's head spun as he tried to sort out the images of bare asses being spanked, more naked breasts than he'd seen in his life and some of the other weird stuff he'd watched.

And another part of him was very aware of the woman at his side. He wondered what she was thinking.

Right at that moment, though, he couldn't find the words to ask. He simply walked beside her, hearing only the sound of the gravel as it crunched beneath their feet. Perhaps words weren't even necessary at this point—he didn't know.

There was so damn much he still didn't know, still didn't fully understand about the whole BDSM scene. He felt like he'd just scratched the surface. And he never did check to find out what those swing things sold for.

They crossed the stones to the hotel back entrance and went inside, climbing the stairs together and eventually stopping outside Tracy's room.

He reached out and put a hand on hers just as she was about to put her key in the door. "Are you sure about this? *Really* sure?"

He had to ask. *Had* to know that in spite of how little they both knew, they were still on the same page—still wanting to explore the same things together.

She stilled, hand on the key. Then she looked up at him. "Yes, I'm sure. I'm very sure. I'm tired of the usual stuff—what do they call it? Vanilla?" Her lips curved in a little grin. "Vanilla doesn't do it for me anymore. I need to know what it's like to totally let go. To not worry about stupid things. To—to—*submit*." She swallowed. "You know what I mean."

"I think so." He lifted his hand away and she unlocked her door. "You want to try some strawberry?"

He followed her inside. "Last chance, Tracy." He stood by the still-open door. "Once I close this door, things change between us."

She put her keys on the little shelf and turned to him. "I know." She straightened her shoulders and slowly lifted her hand to her shirt. "We should have a safe word, George. Will you pick one for me?"

"You think we'll need it?"

"I don't know. Probably not, but then again—I really don't know." She looked confused for a moment or two. "There's a hell of a lot I haven't been able to figure out yet. But I did catch on that we should have one anyway. Just in case? That whole SSC thing that Amy told me about…"

"Yeah. Damien mentioned it." George nodded. "Okay. Our safe word…" He paused and thought for a moment. "*Aruba.*" A place he'd always wanted to visit, to run away to, on occasion. A place he equated with the ability to leave all his worries behind and step outside reality. Someplace he figured he could probably get laid on a deserted beach if he wanted to. It seemed appropriate for this moment.

"*Aruba.* Got it." Tracy sighed softly. "Wonderful choice. Now we're good to go." One by one she undid the buttons until the front of her blouse was open, hanging down over her breasts. She wasn't wearing a bra.

Her head fell forward a little and her hair hid her cheeks as she reached for the snap on her pants. Equally slowly she slid the zipper downward. She wasn't wearing panties either.

"I thought—I wondered if you might find this—appealing…"

Her gaze met George's. As he shut them into their own private world, she bowed her head again, a position he'd seen often that night in the dungeon. It was a submissive's way of standing when next to her Dom. "*I'm yours.*"

Chapter Thirteen

Tracy knelt in front of George with her wrists tied behind her back.

They'd both laughed when it turned out each had independently looked at the scarves from the Oriental silks table. George had been very pleased to find out there was a bonus in the bag Jin had given him...a matching black silk blindfold. He'd produced it from his pocket with a wicked grin playing around his lips, which told Tracy without words he was thinking up some interesting things to do with these toys.

And when his gaze flickered to her body, she figured she was starring in some of his fantasies.

"Take your pants off for me, Tracy." His voice was husky as he gave her his first order—his first command. "Take them off but leave your shirt on. Pull it apart so I can see your breasts."

Awkwardly, she'd obeyed him, amazed at the shaky feeling running through her nerves. She'd never actually done this herself—it was usually a natural part of lovemaking. Undressing each other without much thought to it. Now she was practically stripping for a man while he watched.

It was—exciting, in a way. And a bit terrifying too. No wonder her fingers fumbled as she pushed her pants down and kicked them away along with her shoes. What would he demand she do next? It was a mystery and that very element— that *not knowing*—sent a bolt of arousal down to her pussy. She could feel the moisture as it began to gather between her thighs.

"Put your hands together behind you."

Oh God. She shivered as she felt the silk scarf he wrapped around her wrists. He was thorough, making sure she was tightly restrained but not uncomfortable, taking his time to check his knot and straighten out the delicate fabric.

When he was done, she tentatively flexed her fingers. Tracy could move them, even turn her wrists around a little. But there was no question she was tied tight. Helpless.

Once more a shiver coursed over her skin. Her blouse was wide open, her breasts on display along with the rest of her and her hands were secured behind her like a fugitive from justice.

This was what she'd signed up for, this delicious feeling of vulnerability. The knowledge that matters were now completely out of her hands—and in George's. She hadn't anticipated the nervousness though. The sensation of being trapped, caught up in something bigger than she'd imagined.

Then he made a slight sound, no more than an indrawn breath. But it reassured her that she wasn't alone in her arousal. That this whole thing was getting to George too. When he returned to stand in front of her, she couldn't help but notice the bulge in his pants where his cock strained hard at the fabric.

She wasn't sure what he was thinking or feeling, but clearly both of them were on the same page. And it looked like it was chapter one of a hellaciously erotic novel.

Then he had pointed at the carpet in front of his feet. "Kneel, Tracy."

Slowly she obeyed, carefully keeping her balance as she dropped—first to one, then the other knee—and settled her ass back on her heels. Without being told, she once again lowered her gaze to the floor. She couldn't look at him, couldn't risk a glimpse at the expression in his eyes. She was, she confessed to herself, afraid of what she might see.

Lust? Desire? Disinterest? Or worse, nothing at all? It was really strange not knowing how one's partner felt. Tracy realized that she missed that sense of interaction. Without being told, she knew she would remain silent as a good submissive should. Unless specifically permitted to speak, she'd keep her thoughts to herself. And as a matter of fact, she found it wasn't hard. There was too much going on in her head for her to even think of trying to say something.

"Look up at me." George slid the blindfold over her eyes and tightening it with a gentle tug around her head. She was now in the dark, literally as well as figuratively.

She waited.

"Open your mouth."

George looked at Tracy's face as she obediently parted her reddened lips. Without a second thought, he dropped his pants in a clump around his ankles and kicked them away, shucking off his shoes and socks at the same time. His cock was hard and his arousal flooded his body with a furious heat. He had her doing whatever he asked. And it excited the shit out of him.

Slowly George moved his hips forward, letting the swollen head of his cock brush against Tracy's wet lips and closed his eyes as he moved deeper, her mouth enveloping his cock.

"Oh shit. Damn, Tracy, your mouth is so hot." He sighed and slowly moved his torso back and forth, relishing the moist strokes. He opened his eyes, watching his cock disappearing between Tracy's lips. The room was dimly lit but what light there was shone on the saliva along the shaft of his cock as he fucked her mouth. George could watch her lips tightening around him, movements that were accentuated by the shadows dappling her face. Her tongue brushed along the loose skin just below the head of his cock and she made tiny slurping sounds as drool dripped to her chin.

He lowered one hand, reaching behind Tracy's head and guiding her speed. "Oh fuck—*suck*, Tracy. Suck my cock.

Mmmm, suck..." George closed his eyes and let his head fall back, losing himself in the simple pleasure of her mouth.

He sensed her fidgeting a little, squirming and angling her head to take as much of him as she could. He peeked down at her from beneath his eyelids. Her nipples were hard beads jutting from her breasts and he could smell the sweet honey tang of her juices. She sighed and a tiny whimper emerged from her throat.

George moaned, his knees beginning to weaken. "I've been thinking about fucking you all day. Oh *shit*, I'm gonna lose it if I don't stop..."

With a "pop" he pulled his cock from Tracy's mouth and felt his heart pounding hard within his chest. He wanted to fuck her so badly his head buzzed with it, making him dizzy.

She was kneeling, blindfolded, bound tight, with the front of her blouse wide open. Her breasts were perky with nipples begging for his touch. Just the sight of her was enough to make him ache, let alone the scent of her.

One thing kept hammering at what was left of his brain. She was his—*all his*.

He reached his hand down to her shoulder and pushed the shirt away, exposing all of one breast. Carefully he slipped an arm around her, tugging upward and urging her to her feet. She staggered a little, obviously finding it hard to balance with her arms tied behind her body.

George wanted her more than ever.

Tracy stood, lost in darkness, the taste of George's cock still on her tongue. Her arms began to ache a little from holding this unnatural position and the skin on her wrists throbbed. Without realizing it, she'd fought to loosen her bonds, to reach up and grasp that cock, slick her own saliva over its length, slide her fingers over it and around it...

But she couldn't. She'd had to let *him* set the pace between them, to tell her with his hand how to move, how deep, how fast—it was satisfying to know she was doing what he liked best. But it was also frustrating to not be able to see his face as she devoured him.

Tracy wanted to see the heat in his eyes. She wanted to see the flush on his cheeks as she ran her tongue along his ridges and if there was one particular sweet spot that would make his muscles lock in a sensual response. She wanted to catch a glimpse of his expression when he looked down at her, watched her sucking his cock. Would he stare at her mouth? Her eyes? Would he lift his gaze to her hair as he ran his fingers through it to cup it and move her head into the rhythm that he liked best?

George caught her by surprise when he mumbled something about stopping—her mind was so focused on her mouth and his cock, she barely heard the words. It was as if the blindfold had shut down part of her brain, leaving the rest in a heightened state of awareness. Totally lost in the taste and the feel of him, her world had shrunk to include only George and the salty sweet length of flesh she sucked so fiercely.

When he pulled himself free of her lips, she nearly sobbed. Without his velvety skin between her lips, she was adrift…alone in the darkness, aroused but unfulfilled. Tracy caught a breath as she waited, wondering what would come next. For the first time she realized exactly what surrendering control to another meant. Not only would she let go of the reins when it came to fucking, but she would also let go of her own wants and needs.

She'd forgotten her nakedness, suppressed the ache in her empty cunt. Now that she was alone, isolated by her restraints and the blindfold, she sensed the hot moisture seeping from her pussy, the swelling need that made her nipples hard and sensitive to the slightest brush of air. Her skin was alive with the hot tingling trickle of her arousal, even as her legs and wrists ached a little.

Pure Sin

In that moment she learned that submission was a blend of the sweet and the bitter, a tangled mix of heated pleasure and desolate emptiness.

It was a major Zen moment, but it lasted only seconds—then George cupped her breast.

George felt her jerk in surprise as he touched her, and then saw the shudder build beneath his hand. He walked around her, stroking then fondling parts of her body. Neither he nor Tracy knew where his next touch would be.

This was a wonderfully erotic game to George, this toying with her. He loved grabbing her ass or stroking the soft skin of her side just below her breast. He licked his lips, looking at her as if she was a meal for his eyes and body. He wanted a taste. Taking a firm grip on her shoulders, he turned her to face him.

George paused, looking at her breasts, succulent mounds to be devoured. Between her thighs, her pussy was a burning pot of desire in dire need of licking. He leaned forward and let the heat of his breath wash over Tracy's breast. Sticking his tongue out just a little, he flicked it across the erect tip of one nipple.

Tracy couldn't quite hold back a moan, but pushed herself toward him, a silent invitation for him to continue.

"Open your legs wider."

Tracy shifted her position, following his instructions.

George enjoyed this kind of play—sensually teasing a woman. He knew sometimes it was hard for women to take. It excited him to arouse and excite his lover to such a state that any kind of stimulation would set her off. It also got him so hard he could cut steel with his cock. Erotic games worked both ways.

Stepping around Tracy to her back once more, George stripped off his shirt and pressed his bare chest against her. He tugged her blouse lower down her arms, licking her hot flesh as it was revealed. Her muscles tightened and flexed as he kissed and licked her spine. The shirt was now hanging between them, a minor annoyance, so he quickly wrapped it over the ties around her wrists. Now he was free to enjoy himself to the fullest. George reached around Tracy and grabbed her breasts in his hands. Her back and arms pressed against George's chest and the heat between their bodies went from a smolder to a fire. George pulled her hard against him, molding them together.

His mouth found her neck and he kissed her. He could feel her pulse as her heart raced and he gently rubbed her nipples with his index fingers. The blindfold held her hair away from her ears and George took advantage of it. He traced the outer ridge and whispered softly as he teased her body.

"I'm going to fuck you, Tracy. Nothing more and nothing less." He bit on the earlobe and lowered one hand down over her belly. He slowly moved his fingers further until he found the small patch of pubic hair.

"We're going to have to do something about this." He laughed softly as he tugged on her soft curls.

Sliding his fingers between her open legs, Tracy moaned as he began to rub the folds of flesh. "Your pussy is so wet. You're all primed for a good fucking, aren't you?"

Unable to resist the temptation, he raised his hand to his mouth and sucked on the tips, savoring them. "Mmm. Now that's a tasty little pussy you have there."

Tracy bowed her body as George continued toying with her pussy and nipples, aware that she wouldn't speak or ask him to do anything. She was his submissive. She was at his mercy.

But she wasn't completely still. Her bound hands flexed, her fingers finding something she could do. Her hands began to massage what was behind her. George clenched his teeth and continued his play as Tracy massaged his cock past her restraints and the rumpled shirt between them. She wiggled her ass as George kept rubbing on her swollen clit. He could feel the jolts of excitement shooting through her body and wondered if she was doing what he was doing in his head—picturing his cock hammering into her cunt. He felt her skin like a lick of flames, fueled by the desire he was stroking. She was getting closer all the time.

So was he. George was sweating and as aroused as Tracy. With each movement, each brush of their bodies, his cock got harder and harder until he couldn't take it anymore.

George stepped back and grabbed Tracy's shoulders, guiding her into the bedroom. He toppled her face down onto the bed. Desperate to fuck her, he glanced around. His pants were back in the other room, of course, with the supply of condoms tucked away inside his pocket.

Thankfully, Tracy hadn't been unprepared. There were several condoms on top of her bedside table.

With a silent prayer of thanks, he grabbed one and fumbled with it just as Tracy moved to roll over. "Oh no you don't." George moved a hand to hold her in place, exactly where he wanted her.

Reaching beneath her, he propped her ass up and moved her knees apart. Her face was buried into the mattress of the bed, her hands thrust upward to the sky.

George grabbed her ass in both hands and bent down to lick the dripping opening of her soaked pussy. She was helpless, naked and bound, ready for him to take whatever pleasures he desired at that moment. The skin on her buttocks was soft and white, a glowing invitation scented with her unique fragrance.

Tracy moaned into the comforter as George stood up. Unable to resist the temptation, he swatted her ass with a sharp slap, then gritted his teeth and plunged his iron-hard cock into Tracy with one long thrust. He felt his cock strain within her cunt as she moaned again. Almost stumbling, he pulled out then slammed back into her until his abdomen crashed against her. George was panting and blowing out hot bursts of air, trying to catch his breath and stifle the urge to explode.

"Oh fuck, your pussy is so *fucking* hot." George arched back, buried deep into Tracy's boiling heat. Juices dripped along the base of his cock and trickled between his balls.

The loud slap of flesh on flesh echoed in the room as George smacked Tracy's ass once more. A muffled groan rose from Tracy's throat and the bed creaked as her weight lunged forward with each thrust. Her body flexed and moved as George hammered over and over again into her cunt.

This was pure sex—an elemental fucking—without limits. Totally in control of what was happening, George unleashed the male predator within, allowing himself to satisfy his cravings, his desperate need to take everything he wanted from Tracy.

Another slap—and a red handprint burned on her ass.

"Tighten your cunt around my cock, Tracy. I want it tighter." George was drowning beneath the incredible sense of power and nearly crazed by the feeling of command that overwhelmed him at that instant. Everything he'd ever desired or fantasized about was coming to life. He growled as Tracy tightened the walls of her pussy around his strained cock. He knew she was climbing to her peak and needed to come. The tiny whimpers and trembling of her body told him so as clearly as if she'd said the words aloud.

"Oh fuck. How are you doing that? Oh shit, I'm going to come, oh shit—" George groaned as he erupted inside Tracy. Over and over he spewed his seed—he swore he was blowing the top of the condom off with the intensity of his climax. Her cunt milked him with sharply gripping spasms of her inner muscles.

She screamed as they froze, locked together in a shuddering mass of sexual insanity, rolling beneath the waves sweeping them both off the edge and into bliss. Long moments passed—hell, it could've been hours or merely seconds—George had lost track of time.

But finally it eased and staggering backward, George pulled himself out of Tracy's cunt. Sweat beaded across his forehead and he took a deep breath, wiping it from his eyes as it rolled down over his face. Tracy had collapsed onto the bed and was weakly trying to roll over to her side. Taking pity on her limp efforts, George pulled the blindfold off her head then reached behind her and tugged the shirt and silk scarves free of her wrists.

He moved from the bed to the tiny bathroom vanity and once again tried to catch his breath. That had been…fucking *incredible*.

* * * * *

Tracy lay panting on the bed, squinting a little as her eyes readjusted to the light. Cautiously she rubbed the slight soreness around her wrists and glanced into the bathroom, grinning to herself as George fumbled with his sticky condom and a box of tissues. She choked down a giggle as he tried to get the lubricant off his fingers, shaking them and grimacing at them like he had a sticky booger that wouldn't drop away. If he'd been wearing pants he'd probably have done the guy-thing and wiped his hands over them.

Finally clean, he came back into the room and saw her watching him. "You okay?"

She sighed and nodded. "Oh yes. My ass is pretty warm, but yes. I'm *real* okay." It was the truth too. She was still riding the aftereffects of a massively satisfying orgasm, yet able to appreciate the sight of a very naked George. His cock was relaxed, his body damp—she felt the urge to just lick him from head to toe. He'd released something inside her other than his come. For once, she felt free to let herself think about all the things she'd like to do to—and with—this man. All the pleasures that she could derive from being with him.

Other—more pressing—needs made themselves known. "I could use a quick trip to the bathroom myself, if you don't mind."

George grinned. "Sure. Go ahead. I'm not going anywhere."

A few minutes later, Tracy re-emerged, feeling refreshed and tingling with expectancy. Something told her the night wasn't over yet.

She was right.

George was sprawled on the only comfortable chair in the room, an upholstered affair with a matching ottoman on which he rested his crossed legs. Apparently the inn figured guests might want to enjoy a book or their coffee someplace other than the bed.

"I want you to do something for me." He looked steadily at her as she went to sit on the side of the bed next to him.

"Okay."

His expression was hard to read, although Tracy watched his eyes as they flickered over her naked body. He wasn't aroused again—yet—but there was something heated and sensual about his gaze. It was almost a caress and in spite of her recent orgasm, she felt a little spark of sexual interest renewing itself in her cunt.

"I've always wanted to see a woman make herself come. Just the thought of a woman masturbating turns me on. I want you to do it—for me."

Tracy looked at George, apprehension rising in her throat as she absently chewed her lower lip. He was asking for something she'd never done before, since up to now she'd felt that masturbation was a private matter, best kept to times alone in the bathtub with the shower attachment. Or the solitude of her bed at night.

She swallowed, torn between the uncomfortable sense that this was going beyond sex into the realms of intimate personal exposure and the little shiver of excitement the

Pure Sin

thought of actually *doing* it produced. It wasn't like he was asking her to go out and come in public—but the feeling that she would be breaking some sort of unspoken taboo persisted.

It was exactly that feeling, that she'd be breaking some rules, that finally drove her to nod her agreement. "Sure. If that's what you want."

As soon as the words were out of her mouth, she wondered if she'd done the right thing. Her skin heated beneath the blush she could feel spreading over her skin, which was pretty damn stupid considering what they'd just done not ten minutes earlier.

Tracy glanced around. "Where…uh…" *God*. How the *fuck* did one ask a guy where he'd like her to masturbate?

"On the bed. Up against the pillows." George got up and moved the chair a little, arranging a front row seat for himself. As she shifted into position, he sat back down. "Do you have any toys with you?"

"Toys?"

"Yeah, you know. A battery-operated-boyfriend. *Bob*." He grinned. "I thought every woman traveled with a *friend* these days, if you know what I mean."

Tracy swallowed. "Well, as a matter of fact…"

Her mind darted to visions of absently shoving her toiletry kit into her suitcase. A friend had given her a *Portable Passion Pack* as a joke one Christmas—and she'd tucked it into her travel supplies without paying too much attention at the time. Since then, she'd tried out a couple of the items, learning that the tiny little vibrator was actually quite powerful. It had become a *close* friend on more than one occasion.

She cleared her throat. "In the bathroom. I do have…um…" *Shit*, even her breasts were blushing and to cover her embarrassment she started to move. "I'll get it…"

"No, sit there. I'll get it." George stood and went into the bathroom.

"It's in the blue bag…" Tracy called after him.

"Got it. What the fuck?" George returned looking with interest at the tiny bullet-shaped piece of plastic in his hand. He poked at it and jumped a foot when it buzzed to life on his palm, dropping it in surprise onto the comforter. "Fuck. That little puppy's got quite a kick."

Tracy bit her lip to hold in her laugh. "Um…yes. It's supposed to. It also has two speeds though. I think you turned it to high."

Cautiously he passed it to Tracy. "Just *high*? Should be *Wowweee*." He resumed his seat. "I can't wait to see you use it."

Her laughter died in her throat as George settled into the chair and stared at her. The air in the room seemed to thicken and she couldn't help but notice his cock stir as she parted her thighs and leaned back into the pillows.

"Show me, Tracy. I want to watch you."

With great deliberation, Tracy turned the vibrator in her hand, finding the small switch and flicking it to low speed. It was no longer than half a finger and barely as wide—something designed specifically for travel and quiet private moments.

This moment, however, was anything but private.

Letting it run quietly for a moment on the bed beside her, Tracy swallowed down her apprehension. "It'll take a few minutes—I'm still kind of-of-*tender*…"

"That's okay. We're not in a hurry."

She nodded, glad he understood.

She could do this. She really *could* do this if she focused hard enough. Even though part of her brain was screaming in abject horror at the mere thought of masturbating in front of a man. Ghosts of private fantasies whirled in her thoughts, but none could match the real-life experience she was about to undertake.

She risked a quick glance at George. He had settled himself more comfortably in the large chair, one knee bent slightly as his feet rested on the ottoman. Tracy saw him swallow. That little ripple in his throat gave her courage.

He wasn't quite as calm as he wanted her to believe. Beneath his cool expression, *something* was going on. Something heated his skin, making his muscles shift slightly as he breathed.

The knowledge helped her open the final door—and touch herself.

Putting the vibrator down beside her, she cupped her breasts, a familiar warmth and shape she knew intimately. They were full, swollen from sex and George's caresses. Her nipples were soft but ripened quickly as she stroked her palms across them, budding into peaks within moments. Sensitive already, her skin grazed them almost painfully and she sighed at the tiny tingles beginning to course through her body to her clit.

Absently, Tracy lifted a hand to her mouth and sucked on two fingers, wetting them then smoothing the cooling saliva over the tender tips of her breasts. Wet and slick, the skin rippled as the air in the room cooled them and her fingers slid more easily over and around them.

She sighed and leaned back a bit more, enjoying the warmly arousing sensation of her own touch. She loved this, these slowly building moments when her body awoke to a knowledge of its sexual capacity and the growing anticipation of what lay ahead.

As she'd supposed, it was slower than she was used to — she'd already come once tonight and the responses of her body were more sluggish. This wasn't going to be a quick five minutes and then lather-rinse-repeat. This was going to be a full-blown exploration of her own steps to orgasm.

She squeezed her breasts together with one hand, playing with both nipples at the same time, then finding one with thumb and forefinger, pinching gently, tugging—doing all the things that gave her exquisite pleasure and helped her arousal build steadily onward.

Tracy risked a quick glance at George. His gaze was fixed on her hands—her breasts—every move she made was being closely watched. His cock had begun to harden, but he seemed impervious to it, so focused was he on her movements.

For a blinding second she felt—naked—vulnerable—more bare than she'd ever been in her entire life. Her hand faltered and paused, but then George blinked quickly and licked his lips.

She was getting to him.

Ready to take the next step, Tracy picked up the little vibrator and slid her finger into the top of it. Designed just for this purpose, it fit snugly, trembling with eagerness to get the job done for her.

With one hand still squeezing a nipple, Tracy slid the other down to her pussy and rested it against the base of her mound.

A sigh echoed through the room, but whether it had come from her or from George, she couldn't have said. All she knew was that the touch of the vibrator in that particular spot had awoken her clit, sent shivers up her spine and electrified the sensation of her fingers on her breast.

She let her finger stay still for a few moments, enjoying the soft thrumming as it spread heat and awareness through her pussy and her clit. This wouldn't be a deep penetrating event—her masturbation never was. She had learned that giving herself the most pleasure came from stimulating herself gently and thoroughly, over her pussy, around the tiny bunch of nerves that lurked beneath a shield of protective skin.

She wasn't an "elevator button" woman. If she didn't come right away, repeatedly pushing the button wouldn't make her come any quicker, information a couple of her less-successful dates could have used to everybody's advantage.

Without thinking about it, she let her head loll backward onto the pillows stacked behind her and closed her eyes. Her thighs shifted farther apart and she began the stroking touches that would fuel her inner fires until they exploded into orgasm.

Familiar with her own body's responses, Tracy began to stroke herself, lost now in the pleasure of the toy and the heat flowing through her cunt like a river rising before a flood.

It felt so fucking—*good*. She'd nearly forgotten about the man watching her.

* * * * *

George shifted in his chair. No matter the position, he couldn't get comfortable. He didn't dare move, though, because he had a front row seat to a long unfulfilled fantasy. This was the best thing he'd watched since his team made the playoffs. His team had lost but he knew for sure that tonight, he was going to score.

His cock was hardening and the urge to grab it intensified. He could picture his cock replacing that small plastic device Tracy was using to pleasure herself. He scooted down in the chair and shifted his legs wide apart, letting the solid flesh rise freely between them into his grasp. His monster wanted to play again.

The soft mechanical buzz echoed through George's head as he stared, looking at the vibrator then at the stiff cock in his hand. His cock was damn sure bigger than that vibe. He heard a soft moan from Tracy's mouth and a shudder of pleasure shot through George in response. This was a definite turn-on for him, a dream he'd never believed he'd ever get to experience in real life.

The sound of the vibrator mingled with the soft noises Tracy was making as her finger slid around her pussy lips. It was an erotic song to which she knew the words. She moaned as a particularly sensitive spot emerged, a place where the merest touch of the toy spawned shivers and juices that leaked over her flesh.

Briefly pulling her hand away, she upped the setting to high. She was near now, near enough to want to take that final step. As she returned her hand to her pussy, she reached down with the other one, spreading her fingers over her mound and easing the swollen folds apart.

She knew this would expose places that were ready to be stimulated, places that would respond with an urgent hunger to the throbbing pulse of the vibrator. And she caught sight of George.

His lips were parted, his eyes staring fixedly at her pussy. His neck fluttered over the pulse that pounded just beneath the skin, a rapid movement that showed her how his blood was coursing through his veins. A tiny trickle of drool slid from the corner of his mouth.

Her gaze drifted lower and she watched him past narrowed eyelids, noting how his hand had found his cock and was stroking it, not roughly or fast as if he was masturbating too, but patiently, maintaining his erection, stimulating himself slowly—adding a physical component to his personal enjoyment of her pleasure.

It was hot, empowering, driving her higher into her own delight.

She was going to come soon—she knew it from the urgency building in her cunt and the soaking moisture wetting her thighs and her fingers as she moved the vibrator over her slippery folds.

Her pussy throbbed, aching now for the moment when she would push herself past the limits, beyond the edge of her body's abilities to hold back. It had been a slow climb at the beginning, but now she was on fire, gasping and squeezing her eyes closed as her world focused down through her belly to her clit.

She shivered and her mouth opened on a silent cry, every muscle taut and straining.

It was coming—she was coming—

"Stop." A hand grabbed her wrist and tore her fingers from her pussy.

George.

Choking a cry of frustration, Tracy jerked her head up and opened her eyes with difficulty. "*What?*"

He was standing next to the bed, already sheathed in a condom, erect and flushed as he held her arm tightly. "Fuck me. *Now.*"

Not giving her a chance to do more than suck in a breath of air, he pulled her across the comforter and collapsed down into the chair, tugging her over his knees and onto his lap, making her straddle him.

Her legs folded down either side of his hips and she stilled, inches above his cock. Her heart thundered, her body trembled and Tracy thought she might go mad if she waited a moment longer.

"Do it. Fuck me, Tracy. And don't be nice about it. Tell me *how* you're going to fuck me then do it." George's voice was rough, his fingers holding her body so tight he was probably going to leave bruises. "Tell me how it feels. Don't hold back, Tracy. Fuck me with your cunt *and* your words…"

His gaze was fierce, his cheeks burning with heat. Tracy felt something inside her loosen and slide free. It was the last of her inhibitions.

"All right. I'll fuck you." She reached down between their bodies and grasped his cock firmly, guiding it to her pussy. "I'm going to rub your cock over my pussy first. I like that. It feels hard and smooth and—good."

She slicked it eagerly through the wetness she knew was flowing freely. "Do you like that? Can you feel my hot cream on your cock?"

George groaned and his hips moved—an involuntary thrust that pushed his cock farther into her grasp and almost past her swollen folds.

"You're ready to fuck, aren't you? Ready to go deep into my cunt—" With a quick downward bounce, Tracy pushed herself onto George's cock. "Deep, just like that. Fuck me, George. You're stretching me. Filling my cunt."

Feverishly, Tracy moved on George's lap. *This* was fucking—*this* was what they both wanted, both needed. This, Tracy realized, was how it should be between a man and a woman.

She let go and rode George—hard.

George's nostrils flared and he sucked in air between his clenched teeth.

"Oh yeah, George, fuck my pussy." Tracy grabbed at George's chin, pulling his head forward and down. "Watch it. See your cock getting sucked into my cunt. You like that?"

Tracy threw her head back. She struggled to keep her balance as she let go of George's face to grip the arm of the chair. Almost unaware of what she was doing, her other hand pulled and tugged at her nipples, pushing her body higher and higher. She was on fire—burning—*free*—

"Fuck me, George. Damn, just keep fucking me…" Her body jerked up and down as she thrust herself onto him, a rhythm that made her feel like a rodeo champion breaking a wild bull. All the tensions of this night were frantically blending to the point where they would snap and send her flying. The dungeon, the blindfolded sexual submission, the way she had brought herself so close to coming only to be stopped at the last second—denied the rush of a mind-blowing orgasm—

George was on the verge of a nervous breakdown. His fantasies were all coming true in one night. All by this woman whose body seeped juices of passion down over the sensitive area between his legs. Her pussy squeezed around his cock with every stroke, releasing him as she pulled back then returning to squeeze him once more. He groaned as his balls tightened.

The sex was intense and passionate. George blinked his eyes, trying to clear the thin film of moisture clouding them. He couldn't hear anything she said because the pounding of his heart practically deafened him. He was gasping for air and staring at Tracy's body arching back, twisting wildly as she rode his cock. He craved her.

Her breasts were swaying and full, their straining nipples beckoning his mouth. A stream of drool rolled along his chin. With a quick lunge his lips locked against one breast.

"Oh fuck, yes, baby, suck that tit. Mmm, lick my nipple, George, tongue it, suck it." Tracy began to shudder as her orgasm rolled through her body. "You're making me come, George—oh God—I'm coming—"

Her words pushed the buttons that sent him over the edge and George whimpered as the muscles of her cunt constricted around his cock. His shuddering balls tightened and his body jerked uncontrollably. With a throaty groan he came again, straining to let loose, over and over. He could feel Tracy's pussy creaming around him and her juices flowing hotly between them.

She lowered her head to his and kissed his forehead. They held each other in a tangled web of limbs. Neither wanted to move, neither wanted to cool the heat between them.

With a heavy sigh, George finally leaned back into the chair, sweat glistening on his chest. Tracy leaned back as well, stretching his softening cock inside her body. He flopped free of her pussy and the juices from their sex spilled onto George's lap.

"I guess you get the wet spot this time." Tracy smiled as she stretched her legs awkwardly, got off his lap and walked into the bathroom.

George sat in a pool of Tracy's come with a sticky condom wrapped around his now flaccid cock. He had just acted out most men's dreams. At a time like this he probably should have made up a profound quote to live by or a gesture of some sort to show his satistfaction. He thought long and hard about what to say.

Tracy flicked the light off in the bathroom and came back into the room, looking at George in the chair.

He spoke the first words that came into his head. "I wonder if we can get a pizza delivered? I'm hungry."

How relevantly profound a statement that was, to be sure.

Chapter Fourteen

It could have been a door slamming somewhere or the birds chirping outside. It could certainly have been the fact that her previously dark room was now much lighter as sunshine seeped through the drapes. Whatever the cause, it was enough to slowly wake Tracy from a solid sleep.

She stretched and yawned, aware as she did so of muscles that were protesting and a distinct soreness around her pussy and her thighs. Several hours of intense sex and a couple of massive orgasms would do that to a girl. She grinned as she rubbed her eyes and rolled onto her back.

She wondered if George's cock was sore too. It damn well should be. That last time, she'd really hammered down on it. Turning her head on the pillow, she opened her eyes—to an empty place beside her.

Oh no, not again.

Tracy made herself a note. Speak to George quite firmly about this business of sneaking off before she woke up. It wasn't frickin' fair, for God's sake. At least he could have hung around long enough for a morning cuddle or two. It wasn't like she was going to hit him up for breakfast in bed.

Her stomach grumbled loudly, reminding her that she hadn't actually eaten anything nourishing in quite some time. And she'd sure had enough exercise last night to require at least a couple of steaks, half a dozen eggs and maybe even a few pancakes on the side.

Mouth watering at the mere thought, she eased her cramped limbs from beneath the covers and set about her morning routine, wondering all the time about George. Where was he? Showering maybe? Still asleep? Rubbing the kinks out of his muscles just as she was doing?

Should she call his room, perhaps, or did that look...*pushy*? Shit. Why the hell the guy couldn't just stay put after they'd fucked their brains out, she had no clue. On her way to the bathroom, Tracy glanced around. He'd taken his clothes—all his clothes—so she didn't have the old "you left your watch behind" excuse to contact him.

Shit shit shit.

The sight that confronted her when she turned on the shower and looked into the bathroom mirror, however, was enough to tell her that maybe it was a good thing George wasn't there.

She looked, not to put too fine a point on it, well and truly fucked. Her breasts had red marks in odd places, there was something that could well have been beard-stubble-burn at the base of her stomach, her ass was definitely still pinkish from spanking and the less said about her hair the better.

Her thighs were still a little sticky besides being sore and she'd taken the top layer of skin off one knee—probably when she got the urge to play cowboy and rope herself a steer on that damn chair.

She grinned ruefully. What the hell did a few aches and scrapes matter against a night of the most fabulous sex in her whole damned life? Almost regretfully she stepped into the shower and washed away the evidence. The scent of sweat and sex and George was replaced by lilacs and lavender and her hair returned to its more normal state of order.

But no shower in the world could wash away her memories. The slight sting of the soap on her chafed pussy would fade, the aches in her thighs would ease and all would return to normal.

Would *she*? Tracy didn't know. There were no answers to that yet. Something significant had happened to her last night—something that had shifted her known universe into new and uncharted galaxies. She dried her hair absently, not even seeing her own reflection in the mirror.

She saw somebody else—the woman she'd become last night. Was that woman who she really was? Or was it simply a woman who'd appeared on the spur of the moment in response to such a massive overdose of kinky sex stuff? Was she going to turn into Tracy Harmon, sexual submissive? Or go back to being Tracy Harmon, one-scoop-of-vanilla-please?

She confessed to herself that too many nights like that would require some increased workouts at her gym if she was going to keep doing crazy things in bed. Strength training perhaps, or extra laps around the jogging track…maybe she should up her cardio-workouts…

Wildly unconnected thoughts slithered in and out of Tracy's mind. She let them—welcomed them—since they distracted her from worrying about the most important thing of all.

Where the *fuck* was George?

Putting the finishing touches to her makeup, she realized she'd have to decide what to do—check out today or stay or…or what? So much depended on what George wanted. "Christ, I really am thinking like a submissive." She chastised herself out loud. Bedroom games were one thing, but when it came to her life, she was still in control. Needed to be in control. *Not* being in control left her restless and definitely irritable.

That irritability found an outlet in packing, something she was going to have to do soon anyway. She'd certainly amassed enough background information on the inn to make some helpful suggestions to Mike if they agreed on a contract for an ad campaign. That could all be done by email.

She'd seen Eleanor—and God bless the woman, with a wedding and a baby both coming along, she had more than enough on her plate at the moment. A phone call would take care of that business, although she'd love to see more of Eleanor at another time.

Decisively, Tracy squared her shoulders. If she didn't hear from George before eleven or so, she'd call him. And then she could plan her travel accordingly. After all, everybody should be up by eleven in the morning. It was damn uncivilized to call earlier, but quite acceptable to call the minute after.

She glanced at her watch as she fastened it around her wrist.

Fuck. *Nine-fifteen!*

After a brief period spent filing her nails, a further ten minutes in front of the mirror tweezing her eyebrows and a futile half-hour repacking her suitcase—twice—Tracy gave up in disgust.

George was haunting her as badly as any victim in a horror movie, only without the chain saw. She couldn't see him or hear him, but she knew he was near. She could feel him in some strange way.

Or maybe she was just hungry.

Tracy called room service and ordered herself breakfast. She could have gone to the little dining room and saved a few bucks. But that would mean not being in her room if George came by. Angry at herself for thinking that way but totally unable to *not* think that way, she drank her coffee, nibbled at the food and realized she might just as well face it. She'd changed overnight from an independent businesswoman to a whimpering idiot better suited to the pages of some sweet romance novel. She was pining for a man.

With a sigh, she leaned against the windowsill and gazed out at the trees bordering the grassy patch behind the inn. There was no avoiding it...George was still there, as real as if he stood next to her. He'd reached someplace inside her last night and not just with his cock.

Together, she and George had gone down a road that was new to both of them, finding the courage and strength within each other to explore, experiment and explode—three words she felt suited their lovemaking perfectly.

They'd agreed they were interested in exploring the world of Domination and submission, together they'd experimented with it—and they'd both exploded. Several times.

Tracy still shivered at the mere thought of her orgasms—massive crashing eruptions quite unlike anything she'd ever felt in bed with a man before last night. She was confused by that—puzzled that her physical responses had red-lined so intensely. Wasn't an orgasm just that? An orgasm? The human body had a set of rules for responding to sexual arousal. It wasn't like she pulled in some intergalactic force from Alpha Centauri when she hit the peaks with George.

So why did it feel that way?

The coffee pot refused to part with anything more than a tiny drizzle when she upended it over her cup. Clearly the hotel gods assumed guests only required one and a half cups to start their engines. Tracy growled. She needed at least three.

Ten twenty-five.

Giving up on the stubborn carafe, she figured it was time to pack away her laptop. She'd check and make sure she had all the email addresses and information she needed in the file dedicated to Mike and the inn.

It would be good for another five minutes or so and there was always a last chance to whip through that on-line puzzle she was addicted to and kill another little chunk of time.

Might as well check email too, although since it was a Sunday…

Tracy,

I hope I didn't startle you by leaving like I did. Call it a moment of panic.

You have to know that within one night you freed passions and fulfilled fantasies that I've been longing to explore. You are an incredible woman.

But in sharing an experience like that, I found I had to do a little soul searching afterward. To be bluntly honest, the BDSM scene scares me. Not that it isn't seductive and really arousing – like when you and I watched that couple in the barn and... I'm getting off track here. Sorry...

The words blurred in front of Tracy's eyes as she stared at the email she'd opened automatically. Blinking, she focused again, a slight ringing in her ears getting louder as she read on.

I guess I'm kind of flustered here. Things are somehow a little fuzzy this morning. I've seen and done things this weekend that most times I thought I'd only see in movies at porn shops. You know, the ones where you pay a dollar for tokens and you keep pumping tokens into them until... I'm giving too much info.

To be honest, I just need a little time to get a grip on things. Everything is going so fast.

I know you understand what I'm trying to say here because you're probably thinking some of the same thoughts too.

George

Tracy's world crashed to a halt. Her vision fogged, her throat closed up and for a few moments she wondered if that crushing pain in her chest was the onset of a heart attack or something.

In a vague state of stunned shock, she closed the email and automatically shut down her laptop. The movements were routine, accomplished without conscious thought. A good thing, since at that moment Tracy was incapable of thinking.

Her mind was totally blank.

George was trying to let her down easy. The words were supportive and polite but the message was clear. He needed "space". He needed "time". He was "confused". What else did he have to say other than "goodbye"? And that stuff about porn films—oh *God*. He thought she was a slut, no question about it. One of those plastic-breasted "stars" who dropped her panties in seconds flat and did whatever she was told without a blink. A nymphomaniac sex-slut. She'd fallen right into bed with him, let him do all those wonderful things to her, only to leave a bad taste in his mouth, apparently.

Holyfuckingshit. A slut. He thinks I'm a slut.

She couldn't remember exactly what else he'd said. The expression "soul-searching" flashed like neon in her mind. "Scares me" was another one. This wasn't a passionate *I-can't-wait-to-get-you-in-bed-again* email. This was a man uncertain of what he wanted. And uncertain about whether what he wanted included Tracy.

Oh God.

The screen was blank in front of her as Tracy laid her head down on her crossed arms and wept.

* * * * *

"Miss Harmon. Leaving us today?" Monty reached in a drawer and shuffled papers beneath the check-in counter.

"Yes." Tracy hoped the makeup she'd carefully re-applied hid the puffy eyelids and evidence of a crying jag. She hated herself for doing it. She hated the emotions that had poured through her like a flood of agony. And above all, at this moment, she hated George for making her feel that way.

"Well, that was short and sweet." Monty raised an imperious eyebrow then tipped his head to one side, his gaze sharp. "You all right then, dear?"

She nodded. "Thank you, Monty. I'm fine. I just need…to go home now."

His face softened. "I'll get you checked right out. Here's the slip. If you'd pass over your card so I can run it through all this mystical electronic wizardry you can be on your way."

Tracy did as he asked, annoyed that her hands trembled a little over her purse.

Lights flickered, her credit card slid effortlessly through Monty's "electronic wizardry" and she was signing the receipt before she knew it. "Thanks. You've got a lovely place here." She pushed the pen and the paper back over the counter.

Monty sighed, tore off her copy and came around the counter with it. "Look, dear." He folded the paper thoughtfully. "I'm an old man with an abrasive attitude sometimes. But I know people. And you're not exactly the happiest of campers this morning, are you?"

Tracy felt herself withdraw as she accepted her credit card receipt. She wasn't comfortable finding out that her emotions could be read so easily by someone she didn't know. "I'm fine."

He took the handle of her suitcase from her and began strolling across the foyer, tugging it behind him like a puppy. "No you're not. Lying is a sin. Bad girl."

"Monty, I..."

"Shh. I don't want to know what happened between you and that young Adonis. I know something did, since you two made enough noise last night to raise the dead."

Tracy froze midstep. *"What?"* She felt the color flood her cheeks in a hot rush. "You *heard* us? Were you listening outside or something?"

Monty drew himself up to his full height of approximately five feet three inches and looked indignant. "Certainly not. I don't *eavesdrop.*" He took a step closer to her and leaned in. "I simply happened to require a nice drop of — of — *tea* late last night. To get to the kitchen I had to pass your door. A lot of other doors too, but yours was the one that emitted a variety of sounds not usually associated with two people playing *chess,* for instance." He raised an eyebrow.

Tracy gulped. "Uh..."

They reached the door and Monty passed her the suitcase handle. Then he patted her on the arm. "Let it go for now, dear. Sometimes the roads we travel have some bloody rough patches. If it's right, it'll happen. If it's not, let it go." He stretched his spine and looked out into the sunshine. "Lovely day. My Millicent used to enjoy days like this."

Tracy followed his gaze, trying to see past the pain inside her heart and simply focus on the blue skies and the scent of the country.

She failed. "I guess."

"You want to leave any messages for the lad?"

"*No*. No, nothing." Tracy was adamant about that. She had absolutely nothing to say to George, not at this moment anyway. She needed some time now, time to get her head back together, time to figure out where to go from here.

And probably time to do some more crying while she was at it.

The sunny scene before her blurred and she desperately tried to hide a sniffle. "Thanks for everything, Monty."

He nodded. "Have a safe trip then."

"I will."

"And come back and see us again."

I sooo don't think so.

* * * * *

"I don't know, Marcus. This was a really weird thing for me."

"Weirder than that girl and her mother in Mexico?" Marcus paused and took a drink from his mug.

Over the coffee he was sharing with Marcus, George shook his head. "That was an alcohol-induced phase. I don't remember most of that trip. I don't even remember the cross-dressing, transvestite cocktail waitress who French kissed me. What is it with me and transvestite men anyway?"

"Um, George? Is there something we need to talk about?"

"Fuck you." He knew an embarrassed grin crossed his face. This had been a good idea, dropping by the bar early in the day. It took his mind off things. After he'd emailed Tracy he was at loose ends...he couldn't go *see* her, since she was probably still sleeping. There was time.

"George, you were always the guy everyone trusted and confided in. Always the responsible person, the most-likely-to-succeed guy, the one we knew we could count on to bail us out of jail."

"Yeah and you took advantage of that in San Diego, if I remember right."

"You're missing the point. Maybe this affair is a way for you to break free from all the things that sort of held you back."

George considered his friend's words. "Maybe...I don't know. I think I fucked up. This woman is so damn hot, Marcus. She isn't afraid of anything. This just isn't my usual type of woman."

"Why, because she lets you call the shots? Dude, I can remember when I'd thank God for a woman like that. I'm lucky now because Jodi and I are on a level playing field. She and I understand each other. I learned the hard way about shit like that with Vanessa."

"But it's all happening so fast. I think I fucked up. What started out as a great piece of ass has turned into more and she's curious about shit I don't know if I'm ready for. Next thing will be me bending her over while I whip her ass with a flogger or something."

The two men stared silently at each other for a long moment.

"And the problem with that is?" Marcus blinked at him.

"Fuck, you know what I mean."

"Yes, I do. I had to take those pictures of Mike and Amy, remember. It was tough when Amy nearly cried and I looked at Mike and he was so nonchalant about it. Then I saw how hot

Amy got. You think those shots in the art show were intense? I have some of her coming, where you can see her... oh never mind."

George stared wide-eyed at Marcus as he described the shoot. "See her *what*? Don't stop now, asshole." He paused and ran both hands through his hair. "You got an ice pack around, by any chance?"

"Look, George, just talk to her. Don't pussy out with this email crap. You have to talk to her, watch her face, see how she's dealing with this. It needs the personal touch, honest. Find out where her head is. Women will surprise you, dude. They always do." Marcus got up from his chair. He reached behind the bar and shoveled some ice into a plastic bag. "Here. Best I can do in the way of an ice pack for your headache. Before you leave, we'll go somewhere and get a big fucking steak. I love Jodi's cooking but with you here I can go out and get myself a fat-ass steak and potato dinner at a hole in the wall and not feel guilty. Besides, it gives us a reason to drink some beer and bullshit some more."

"I think I fucked up."

"I think we established that you fucked up, George...what you need to do is *un*-fuck this up." They looked at each other for a second. "Finish your coffee. No rush. I gotta do some stuff out back." Marcus disappeared into the recesses of the bar storeroom.

George rested the ice pack snugly between his legs and offered up a prayer to the heavens. *Thank God for ice.* He cooled the ache in his balls as he sat in the dim light for a while, thinking.

What should I do? I left abruptly, kinda snuck out – should I make something up?

Why is it transvestite men always pick me to kiss?

If a guy takes Viagra and his dick never goes soft, would a woman take him to the doctor right away or wait a week?

George shook his head, drained the last of his coffee and dragged his mind back to the problem at hand. *Tracy*.

She was all over him like white on rice. He could still smell her on his skin even after he'd showered. He could still feel her beneath his hands and his body. Still taste her unique flavor in his mouth along with the mint of his toothpaste. She'd sneaked under his defenses and poked her fingers and her lips and her tongue into places no other woman had touched.

Metaphorically speaking.

There was really nothing else to do at this point but follow Marcus' good advice. He really needed to see her, to talk to her. To get stuff sorted out between them and figure out what came next. But first he had to pee.

He glanced at his watch. It was nearly eleven. She should be waking up soon—if not already awake. If he headed back to the inn, he should be just in time to catch her and eat her out for breakfast, or take her to breakfast.

The sunshine glared down on the car as he drove the short distance back to Purett's Inn and Tracy. George banged on his dashboard, playing impromptu drums along with the radio and some old rock song that he vaguely knew.

Life was pretty good at this moment. He'd gotten the sex of his dreams last night, Tracy was at the inn and he'd see her shortly—they'd talk about stuff, sort it all out—if he could persuade her to stay on for a bit—well *shit*. Who knew what they could find to pass the time?

A wicked grin curved his lips and George glanced at himself in the rear view mirror.

Look out, Tracy. Your dreams are about to come true.

Again.

Chapter Fifteen

"What do you mean, *she's gone?*" George gaped at Monty across the shining expanse of counter.

"I mean exactly that. She's gone. Gone as in *no longer here*. If you're planning on playing Prince Charming—forget it. There's no foot around for you to put the glass slipper on."

"How can she be gone?"

Monty sighed. "The same way as everybody else. She came downstairs with her luggage, paid the bill and walked out the front door." He wrinkled his nose. "Not a terribly difficult concept to grasp, you know."

"She's really gone?"

"Yes."

George gaped at Monty.

Who sighed more loudly. "Exactly what part of Y-E-S, *yes*, are you having difficulty with?"

"She *can't* have left." None of this conversation was making any sense to George. It wasn't remotely possible that Tracy would leave before he could talk to her. It just couldn't be happening.

Monty shrugged. "Apparently she never considered such an accomplishment beyond her abilities." He paused and stared at George. "In other words, you twerp, you buggered it up royally."

"Huh?"

"I'm going too fast for you, aren't I?"

"Look." George leaned on the counter. "I was going to spend time with her this morning. I'm going to talk to her.

Talk, you know? We have stuff to work out. Things to-to *talk* about."

Monty nodded. "Got it. Talk. I understand the word, you know. To talk, as in to engage in useful conversational discourse."

George swallowed. "Whatever."

Monty leaned forward, resting his forearms on the polished wood. "All right. I'm going to say this very slowly for you. She…is…no…longer…staying…at…the…inn." He paused once more. "Have I made myself clear now?"

George shook his head in denial. "I don't understand."

"I've failed dismally, haven't I? Should we try words of one syllable? Charades? Morse code?"

George fought down a vicious lump of bile that threatened to choke him. "Monty, I *get* that she's left. I *don't* get *why* she left." He glanced at the old-fashioned pigeon holed mail slots behind the desk. "Did she leave me a message or anything?"

"No." Monty shook his head. "And I did ask too, as a matter of fact." He idly flicked a tiny bit of dust off the counter. "Face it, lad. She's run for the woods. Gone and left you high and dry. Not terribly happy when she left either. Looked a bit glum if you ask me."

"Glum?"

"Yes, glum. Glum as in down-in-the-mouth. Knackered."

George raised an eyebrow.

"Knackered as in…tired. Exhausted. Drained." Monty shot a questioning look at George. "What the *dickens* did you do to her last night?"

"I—" George bit off the sharp response to that incredibly intrusive question. He wasn't about to discuss his and Tracy's sex life with a tall midget, British accent or not.

"Never mind. I'll figure this out. Thanks anyway." George turned on his heel and headed upstairs to his room.

His mind was spinning helplessly, wondering why the hell Tracy had gone without a word. No goodbye, no thanks for the spanking, no God-that-was-the-best-sex-of-my-entire-life.

Maybe she'd left him an email? Perhaps her cat was sick…she'd had some sort of family emergency or something…there could be any number of reasons why she'd had to leave. He couldn't begin to guess at them, but George knew one thing for sure. It hurt. It hurt that she'd gone without a word, a note—a message of any kind.

And underneath all his rationalization, a nasty suspicion grew until it threatened to swamp him and blow off his ears.

He'd fucked up.

Two seconds on his laptop told him there was no response from Tracy to his email. Moments later he was reaching for his cell phone.

"Hey, Marcus…" He stared blindly at his flickering screen. "Sorry to bother you, dude—do me a favor?"

God bless friends.

"I need to know if Tracy spoke with Eleanor this morning and I don't have her number…" This was going to lead to questions, sure as shit. "Yeah, she's checked out. I missed her. I need to touch base with her. I think." He listened to Marcus. "Thanks. I appreciate it. I'll have my phone with me."

Snapping it shut, George pondered his next move. Should he call Tracy himself? Did he even have her cell phone number someplace? He couldn't think, couldn't remember if she'd written it down, or if she had, where he'd put it.

His mind was half-chaos, half-blank, filled with the only litany that made sense at this moment…*I fucked up…I fucked up…*

Somewhere, somehow, someplace along the line, he'd done something or said something that had turned this whole wonderful weekend from sugar to shit in seconds flat and driven Tracy away from him.

That was not what he'd wanted, not what he'd planned when he'd sent her his email. He wasn't even sure himself what he'd been trying to say—he only knew that when he'd woken up next to her this morning, he'd been scared for the first time in his life. Scared that this woman meant more to him than any other woman ever had and that if he wanted her, he was going to have to go places he wasn't comfortable with.

Wasn't he supposed to be honest? Didn't the rules say a guy could share stuff like this with a special person? Weren't those women's magazines full of crap about revealing one's innermost thoughts and emotions to each other? All those ads with hot women telling their innermost sexual secrets. Wasn't he supposed to show sensitivity and his feminine side?

Obviously those writers were blowing smoke out their asses. Something he'd said—or worse, something he'd *done*—in the course of exploring an alternate sexual lifestyle, had sent Tracy running from him.

Maybe he'd been a lousy lay.

Nah...she'd come several times. It *couldn't* be that.

Could it?

Everything replayed in his head. Nothing seemed wrong.

Maybe Tracy felt she'd got too close and really just wanted a weekend tryst in the sack. Maybe she was really hiding the fact she was married with three kids and a fat overweight truck-driving husband who didn't show any appreciation for the way she slaved at home, keeping the place clean *and* being a supermom, taking the kids to ballet classes and soccer practice.

Maybe she was really setting him up to murder her husband and free her from her terrible life. Then he'd end up butt sore from getting raped in prison because she'd woven him into her web of deceit and he took the rap for murder. Of course, she'd leave him for her lesbian lover—the one with a fetish for whips and strap-on black dildos.

What the fuck am I doing? I'm overthinking everything.

Tracy said she wanted a no-holds-barred sexual weekend. Pretty much all holds — and most holes — were used, so maybe she really had just taken what she wanted from George and split.

His cell phone chimed and he grabbed it in a rush. "Hello? Oh Marcus…yeah, how'd you make out?" His spirits fell. "Nothing, huh? Well, thanks for checking." He paused. "I guess so. I'll be checking out in a bit."

Marcus' voice was quietly reassuring against George's ear, a low hum of words that somehow made it into George's confused brain.

"I sure hope so. But I don't really know what I'm going to do next. I gotta figure that out. Yeah, I'll let you know. Thanks for everything, buddy."

Fuck, fuck, fuck.

Eleanor hadn't heard from Tracy. There were no leads, no indication that she'd done anything other than what Monty said. *Gone.* Left George alone with his memories and a strange pain that was seeping through his body, coming to rest somewhere suspiciously close to his heart.

Hanging his head and sighing, George began to stuff his bags messily with his clothes, figuring he might just as well leave town before he tore himself apart. There wasn't anything keeping him at the inn anymore.

He had no cell number, no address, no way to contact Tracy except for email and that was way too impersonal for the conversation he wanted to have. Wait…what did he do with the card she'd given him? He tore out all his not-very-carefully packed clothing and went through it, shaking it, turning out the pockets, even checking inside his socks. One never knew where a small thing like a business card might end up.

But he came up empty-handed with nothing more than a mess of clothes needing repacking again. Depressed, he did just that, shoving them more or less into some kind of order in his case. He was going home empty-handed, leaving with little more than a reconnection to an old friend. And some indelible memories.

One last dinner with Marcus and he'd be gone—he never passed up a free steak dinner along with a few beers. He probably wouldn't be great company but at least he could let Marcus know where he'd be once he got home. That way, if Marcus heard anything at all—from Eleanor especially—he could pass the information along to George.

It was all he could do.

* * * * *

Home was a familiar haven of comfort Tracy burrowed into like a rabbit looking for safety. Her pain eased a little as the door slammed behind her and not long afterward, the pleasure of being back in her own little world helped a couple of aspirin deal with the nagging headache.

She wished she could banish George from her head as easily, but it was gonna take more than a pill or two to get rid of *him*.

Late that night, with a glass of wine beside her and her comfy jammies hugging her chilled body, she admitted that even if she could, there was no way she'd kick George out of her memories. They were too bittersweet and they'd changed her, she knew. This weekend, sharing what she'd shared with him, doing the things they'd done—well, they'd taught Tracy a lot about herself.

She tried to objectively review what she'd learned, only to start shivering at the remembered passion between them. *Shit.* What had she done that had made him pull away from her?

Where had she fucked up? Where had she left the impression she was a slut? Or worse?

Where had she made the one wrong move that had sent George walking backward, away from her? Something she'd said, maybe? She snorted at that idea. They hadn't exactly talked a lot last night.

Tracy ached. This wasn't the simple twang of overextended muscles; this was a soul-deep ache of a woman lost in a maze of questions to which she had no answers.

All she'd wanted was to be with George, to explore new things, try new things—to let somebody else take control for a change. To leave all the decisions in somebody else's hands and just *submit*, to put her inhibitions aside and be free to indulge his wants, knowing she'd satisfy her own in the process. That wasn't being a slut…was it?

There was *one* certainty in all this though. Tracy would never be the same again when it came to sex—and possibly relationships.

She'd *let go*—once—and found more pleasure than she'd realized was humanly possible. It had been the right place, the right time…and the right man. Whether it would ever happen again, she didn't know. But now she had a benchmark, something to measure all her other relationships against.

Deep down inside, she wondered if they'd ever come close to what she and George had shared.

Sure, they'd spent a lot of time immersed in a strange new world of sexual possibilities. They'd learned about practices and pleasures she'd only vaguely dreamed about. Something like that…well, it was bound to put them both in the right frame of mind for hot sex.

They'd certainly fulfilled that part of the deal. Tracy still blushed at the thought of what she'd done while George watched. And yet even as she pressed her cold palms against her hot cheeks, she knew she'd do it again at the drop of a hat.

For George.

Her mind blanked for a moment then shifted as she considered that idea. Perhaps it wasn't so much about the Domination and submission thing. Perhaps the dash of submissiveness hadn't been the focus of her night. She'd let go, let George take the reins, done whatever he'd asked—but she'd done so willingly and enthusiastically and reaped the rewards.

Perhaps—perhaps—it was more about *George*.

Oh fucking shit.

Tracy gulped. Could she have done *any* of the things they'd done if she'd been with somebody else?

Could she have willingly passed over control of her body to another man under the same circumstances?

Could she have gotten seriously turned on by having her hands restrained and her ass smacked—hard—if it had been another man?

Could she have masturbated freely and with a kind of self-conscious pleasure in front of any other man she could think of?

Her wineglass was empty, her feet icy in the darkness. But Tracy ignored these things as she discovered a frightening truth and stared it full in the face.

It was *George*. His smile, his goofball humor, his willingness to listen and to share—the sex had been incredibly wonderful because it was with the *right man*, not because it was the *right type of sex*.

Any kind of sex would have been great with George. Simple, complicated, missionary, Kama Sutra-style, whatever…it would all be fabulous with George, Tracy knew.

And asking herself why that was so…shit, that led places she'd never expected to think about, let alone experience. In the course of not much more than forty-eight hours, Tracy Harmon had done the unthinkable.

She'd gone and fallen in love. It was impossible, unbelievable and totally unreal.

Oh crap. And I've lost him. What the hell do I do now?

What she did, of course, was what any twenty-first-century woman with her own business would do—she *worked*.

Starting the very next morning, Tracy threw herself back into her job with a ferocity that surprised even her. She finished two business plans, contacted several potential clients and went out of her way to locate more.

The days passed in an exhausting haze of emails, phone conferences, the occasional business lunch and more emails.

She absolutely refused to allow herself the luxury of indulging in thoughts of George, although he still remained at the back of her mind, a sensual presence that she knew could make her shiver if she allowed him out to play.

She wasn't a slut, she reminded herself. He needed time to think, she also reminded herself. Well, he'd have it. He could have all the fucking time he wanted. She wasn't about to call him, email him or even try to find his phone number.

She unpacked every piece of clothing she'd taken with her and had it dry-cleaned or laundered. She bought new shoes—a mammoth and expensive splurge she allowed herself by insisting that shopping was the universal panacea to whatever ailed a woman.

The only reminders she couldn't bear to tuck out of sight were the two silk scarves. She'd draped them over the post at the foot of her bed and there they stayed. Whether they served as a reminder of George, or a reminder to Tracy never to be such a complete and uninhibited idiot again, she wasn't sure. But they were there…and after a week or two, they became less of an accusation and more of a gentle memory of a weekend that she would never be able to forget.

Not that she needed it, of course. Drinks with her girlfriends produced the inevitable conversations about men and the occasional pick-up attempt or two. It didn't take much for Tracy to see George's smile in her head. She kept silent about her love life and brushed off invitations to dinner. She just wasn't interested in dating anybody right now and had no inclination to spend an evening with a man she couldn't care less about.

Sleeping with anybody else was totally out of the question. It seemed that George might well have accomplished that incredible achievement of spoiling her for anybody else.

She hoped that would pass. She didn't want to spend the rest of her life alone, comforted only by memories. Finally, nearly three weeks after she'd visited Purett's Inn, Tracy sat down to complete the business plan for Mike.

And the images swamped back into her brain and her heart—a tide of emotional passion that rocked her in her chair. She couldn't concentrate on the numbers, couldn't even make her usual precise language work right.

Eventually she gave up and reached for her phone.

"Hi, Eleanor?"

"*Tracy.*" It was a shriek on the other end of the line that nearly deafened her. "I'm so glad you called, honey. I've been worried about you."

Tracy ran her hand through her hair. "I'm sorry, honest. I didn't mean to just hit the road like that without saying goodbye, but I knew you weren't in top shape—how are you feeling, by the way? Did I call at a bad time?" She glanced at the clock. It was a little past seven at night.

"No, no." Eleanor reassured her. "Justin's at the bar. I used to go with him most of the time, but now I get tired real quick. He's got into the habit of sending me home after he's fed me. And to tell the truth, I'm good with that. Don't have the energy to make it to closing time anymore." She took a breath. "But other than that, everything's fine with me and the baby. Tell me about *you*...what you've been doing...why you left?"

Tracy sighed. "God, El. I don't know where to start. I've been real busy since I got home. Business is booming—I picked up seven more clients in the past couple of weeks—haven't really had time to turn around. I actually got four tentative business plans put together too and used that hot new server—"

"Tracy." Eleanor's voice was calm but decisive. "I'm glad business is good. But that's not why you called me, is it?"

"Huh?"

"Sweetie, I have a sister. I know that tone of voice. Tell me all about it? All about *him*?"

Tears flooded Tracy's eyes and she sniffled, desperately grabbing for a tissue with her free hand. "Noooo." Okay…that was definitely a wail.

"Oh honey. You hurt, I can hear it. What happened?"

Slowly, haltingly, the story of Tracy's wild weekend emerged. And at the end of it, George's email. Blowing her nose hard, she stopped at that point. "So there it is, El. I'm an idiot once more."

"Bullshit." Eleanor sounded crisp. "First off, you still got his email?"

"Umm…well, I was going to delete it, but for some stupid reason I didn't. I did block his IP addy. But I kept that one. I guess I figured it would serve as an embarrassing reminder of what an ass I'd made of myself."

"Read it to me. Word for word. *Now*."

"Yes, ma'am." In spite of her tears, Tracy had to smile at Eleanor's starched schoolmarm command.

Throat clogged, Tracy began to read, aching anew as the words poured from her screen into her heart, leaving bloody tracks as she spoke them into the phone. "So there you have it. The entire brush-off of the biggest slut in the western world." Tracy tried for a little humor.

There was a huge sigh on the other end of the line. "You don't know very much about men, do you?"

"Pardon?"

Eleanor was silent for a second or two. "Look, Trace. This wasn't a brush-off, honey."

Tracy blinked. "Yes it was."

"No it wasn't." Eleanor spoke slowly and patiently, which was a good thing, since Tracy's ears were thrumming a little and she thought she'd heard Eleanor say it wasn't a brush-off.

Sure enough, she repeated herself. "It wasn't a brush-off, Tracy."

"Then what the fuck *was* it?" *It had to be a brush-off. Of course it was a brush-off.*

There was a huge sigh on the other end of the phone. "Tracy, this is a guy's attempt to explain his feelings. Need I say more?"

"I think you'd better. I don't understand."

Another gusty sigh. "Okay, here's the thing. Men don't do emotions well. They do *talking* about their emotions even worse. If there's one thing in this life you can hang your hat on, it's that a man will express his feelings badly — and that's if he does so *at all*."

Tracy swallowed. "All right. I'm with you so far…"

"So you need to take George literally here, honey. He *did* need time to sort out what he was feeling. Give the guy credit for telling you something honest — he loved the whole night he spent with you but wasn't into the BDSM thing. That's surprisingly blunt, no diddling around the topic — it's right out there."

"But…but…that whole porn thing…"

Incredibly, Eleanor laughed. "You sure fulfilled his fantasies from the sound of things, Tracy. But fantasies are just that — fantasies. George wanted time to sort the fantasy from the reality. He's also asking, in a delightfully masculine roundabout kind of way, whether you could still enjoy a relationship with him *without* that BDSM stuff. At no time does he call you a slut. *You* created that image in your mind, since that's how *you* think of porn stars. Most women do." She paused. "Men don't."

"They don't?"

"No. Well, maybe. I'm not sure. But they do seem to spend a lot of time fantasizing about putting themselves in between two of 'em. Justin told me that, once upon a time."

"Uhh...were you pissed?"

"Not really." Eleanor sounded quite calm. "I'd just told him about one of my fantasies. A movie star and a night on the French Riviera."

"Oh."

"So I suggest you re-read that email a couple of times, sweetie. Try to take your own emotions out of the equation when you do. Read his *words*, not what *you* think he was trying to say. Remember, men are simple critters when all's said and done. Odds are good that George simply said what he meant. You *interpreted* it from your point of view, which was totally screwed up with adrenaline, blooming love and the aftermath of incredible sex. Plus a healthy spoonful of confusion about the whole submission thing."

She was silent for a moment. "Am I right?"

This time it was Tracy who was silent as a whole army of new thoughts paraded quick-time through her brain. "Uhhh..."

"I know. It's difficult to figure all this shit out. Justin and I had some real problems too before we finally worked it all out. But we *did* work it out, Trace. If the feelings between you two are real, you'll work it out as well. One way or the other."

Tracy blew her nose. "I fucked up, didn't I?"

"Yep. Big time."

"Well, thanks for the support."

Eleanor giggled. "Honey, there's no such thing as a love affair without fuckups. It's part and parcel of the whole deal. We're human. Thus we're imperfect. It can be fixed."

"I fucked up. I can't *believe* it. I fucked up sooooo badly too." Tracy shook her head, stunned at the revelation. "Here I've spent the last couple of weeks burying myself up to my eyebrows in work so I wouldn't have to think about the bastard and now it turns out he's not such a bastard after all."

"And life goes on. What's more important is what you do next."

"Um, Eleanor? What do I do next?"

"Jesus. I'm not your patron saint, ya know."

"But..." Tracy whimpered. "I don't know how to fix this, El."

"What do you want?"

A simple question, just four little words—and there was no other answer she could honestly give. "I want George."

"Then go get him, sweetie."

"Just like that?"

"Just like that."

* * * * *

It might have been simple to Eleanor, but for Tracy it was the hardest thing she'd ever set out to do.

Heartened the next morning by finding an email on her system offering her two hundred dollars off a trip to *Aruba*—and realizing this was a sure sign from the cyber-gods that she was doing the right thing—Tracy began the slow process of finding a phone number for George. Her email program had obligingly blocked George's communications—if there had been any. It had also apparently wiped him off the face of the planet.

Of course, given his name, every search engine refused to believe she'd spelled it correctly and suggested politely she check it, replace the "U" with two "OO"s and try again, since there were something like twelve million sites with lots of information about the *other* George.

She sighed and gave up for a bit—she had, after all, drummed up huge amounts of work for herself that wouldn't wait.

But later that day she found a local community information site and her hand froze over her mouse as she read the "Weekend Fun" listings. *Wouldn't you know it?* Her jaw dropped as she saw an ad for a new show at the very gallery where she and George had first met. It seemed like a lifetime ago now, but she could recall every single detail.

She grinned as she remembered his cheer for his football team. Then there was that odd look of distaste that had come over him when that woman he was with at the time had barged in. God, what a *bitch* she was too.

Okay. This would be it. From the list of exhibitors, she just knew George would be there. Marcus was listed as having some new prints on display. What more did she need?

Well, clothes, of course. And she was close to running out of shampoo. And...

Tracy's nerves grew from butterflies in her stomach to massive cargo transport planes by the time Friday rolled around and she got to her final shopping. Lost in her own private torment, she nearly ran down the woman in front of her at the checkout line.

"God, I'm sorry. Did I hurt you?"

"No, dear. I'm fine. You must have been miles away though." The woman looked at her curiously.

"Yeah. Sorry. Thinking about George Cluny." *And wasn't that the truth?*

The woman's gaze flickered to the cover of a garish tabloid where a photo of a certain movie star smiled handsomely out at customers waiting in line. She sighed. "Say no more. He gets my juices flowing too. That smile...those eyes..."

Tracy grinned and let her keep her illusions. If all went well, she'd have her own personal hunk of gorgeous.

Standing in front of her mirror the next afternoon, in preparation for her shower, Tracy checked off her list of "todos". Armpits were clean. Legs were waxed and she'd painted her toenails.

A manicure a few days ago was still in good shape, as was her haircut. Thank God there were a few things she didn't have to worry about. Then her gaze drifted to the neat triangle of hair between her thighs.

Hmm. Something George had said popped back into her mind and she turned the idea over for a little while.

"Hell, why not?" Bravely, Tracy marched into the bathroom and grabbed her scented shaving lotion, followed by a new razor.

Within moments, she was staring at herself, awed by the bare pinkness she'd revealed with a few firm swipes of the blade. Delicately, she touched the skin with a finger, amazed at how sensitive it was. She blinked, unable to look away from this most private of places—a slit in her skin where two parts of her body touched over the womanly secrets she knew hid beneath. It was—*surprising*. Strange, yet erotic.

Tracy decided she rather liked it, this feeling of utter nakedness. She sincerely hoped it would meet with George's approval. If he got to see it, of course. That would mean he had come home with her. That would also mean he was actually *at* the gallery.

Shit. She squeezed her eyes shut. Too many variables in the equation. She shrugged. What was done was done. If nothing happened tonight, it would grow out again. She had to stop dithering and just get ready to do this. To go and see if she could find the one man who'd touched so much more than just her body.

If she found him, *then* she'd figure out how best to show him her freshly denuded pussy.

She let that thought sustain her right up until she reached the door of the gallery.

Then, and *only* then, she started to tremble.

* * * * *

George strolled the length of the gallery for the third time. She still wasn't there. But somehow, he had the strongest feeling she'd show. It had taken him a while to get over his anger at himself and come to terms with his own stupidity — whatever it was.

He hadn't gotten over his need for Tracy.

Refusing to resort to pumping his friends for her phone number, George had waited patiently. She had his email address. He hadn't emailed her, figuring the next time they spoke to each other it should damn well be face-to-face. Otherwise history might repeat itself and he'd fuck up *again*. Of course, she might have deleted the darn thing. Finally, unable to stand it, he'd persuaded a buddy of his to send out a "mass" mailing to local residents about the upcoming show at the gallery. It had taken nearly four long weeks to figure the whole deal out, but now it was here — the show was under way, Marcus' new photos were on the wall and George was ready.

There was only one small thing missing — Tracy.

Then the door opened and George's heart skipped a beat as he watched her walk in.

She'd come.

She looked around nervously, he thought, her eyes flickering around the large room. He dodged behind a pillar, not quite ready to say hello until he'd made sure she'd come alone.

Since nobody else entered behind her, he figured he was okay. With a sigh he followed her, finally stopping behind her as she stood staring at one of Marcus' best photos.

He took a breath. "I knew I'd find you here."

Tracy spun around on her heel, a smile lighting her face. Her mouth moved for a moment or two before the words came out. "I saw that Marcus had given more photos to a new exhibit." She let her smile widen as her gaze devoured his face. "I couldn't miss the chance to see them."

"Tracy, I..."

"George, please..."

They both paused then laughed as they realized they'd spoken simultaneously.

She dipped her head and peeked at him from beneath her eyelashes. "You first."

"Tracy, I don't know what happened. I don't know what I said or did." George shifted his gaze to the photo, afraid to look into her eyes.

"God, George, I'm sorry too. It took me a while and a couple of re-readings of your email to calm me down a bit. Now, at last, I understand what you meant."

"My email? My *email* is why you left?" He looked at her at last, realizing she was blushing and not meeting his gaze.

She nodded. "I took it as a brush-off. I was pretty messed up that weekend. We went places that totally turned my world upside down." She turned to him. "Feeling the way I did about everything we did together...I...well, I couldn't *bear* you thinking of me as loose and slutty or something. I'm not *like* that, really. I never..."

"Tracy, shut up. Please. Just be quiet for a moment." His eyes locked with hers and he rested his forefinger across her lips.

"I'd never met anyone like you, Tracy. You gave me your honesty and you gave me your incredible body. I'm already getting a chubby just standing here with you. But more than that, you gave me your *trust*. And I—like the fucking idiot I am—I left you alone afterward with only an email for explanation. I'm a *moron*."

Tracy's eyes gleamed as they filled with tears. "I don't know what to say."

"I was wrong to not stay and tell you face-to-face that I just needed to catch my breath—the breath you took away, Tracy. I got scared. I'm so sorry if I hurt you in any way." George moved his hand and brushed back a few strands of Tracy's hair that had fallen loose across her cheek. She was so beautiful, just standing and looking at him.

"I was frightened too, George. I've never gotten so close to a man so quickly. I was afraid I had scared *you* off." She paused. "And then there was the whole bondage thing tossed into the mix. I've never been more confused in my life." She lowered her gaze. "I loved that part of it, don't get me wrong. But I don't *need* it. I can live quite happily for the rest of my life without having my hands tied behind my back. The one thing I did learn though…the one thing I do need?" She lifted her chin. "I need *you*."

George wanted to shout and punch his fist high in the air. He didn't do either, though, since it might have gotten him thrown out of the gallery. He just answered from his heart. "I need you too."

Tracy sighed and he saw her body relax at his words. She lifted an eyebrow. "Have you been with anyone since that weekend?"

"Yes. I have"

An expression of pain darted across her face.

George smiled and held up his right hand. "I'm surprised I don't have hair all over my palm from thinking about you *every* night."

Tracy looked at George, her heart in her eyes. "I'm glad. I couldn't even see anybody else, let alone date them." She turned toward the picture on the wall and slowly leaned back against him. "So what do we do now?"

"I think…" He nuzzled her ear. "That we have some talking to do, followed by some pretty intense making up?"

"Mmm. I like the sound of that."

"Let's get out of here." George briefly hugged her.

"Okay."

Tracy slipped her arm through George's as they headed to the door. "Oh and I've got something I really want to show you. You talked about it, once upon a time."

"Really? What?" George tilted his head at her.

Her grin was beautiful, joyful and incredibly naughty. "You'll see."

Epilogue
Much later that same night…

ಬ

With a thump, George fell flat onto the bed, his chest sweating and heaving as he gasped for air. He listened for a few moments to his heart, which pounded like a heavy metal rock band doing an encore after their best show ever.

He was back where he belonged, in Tracy's bed and in her life. He planned on staying there for a while too. A slow growl rumbled from his stomach. "Chinese food sounds good. I wonder if they deliver?"

She was beside him, limp, boneless and damp, sprawled over the tangled sheets with her bottom curling in to his body. Life, thought George at that moment, was fucking *perfect*.

"What is it with you and food after sex?" Tracy stirred and sat up.

"You okay?" George opened a sleepy eye.

"Yeah. I'm cold. Just going to pull up the sheets."

"Okay." George closed his eyes again, only to jerk them wide as he felt something wrap around his ankle.

He lifted his head curiously from the pillow. "What the fuck…?"

Tracy ignored him, continuing to loop the silk scarf from the dungeon fair around *both* their ankles.

"What the *hell* are you doing?"

She finished her task, straightened the elegant bow then flopped back beside him, bringing the covers and a huge smirk with her.

"Tracy?"

"Yes?" She chuckled and snuggled close. "Just this once, I'm gonna make damn sure I don't wake up *alone* tomorrow morning. Got it?"

George grinned and settled her into his arms. "Got it."

Why an electronic book?

We live in the Information Age—an exciting time in the history of human civilization, in which technology rules supreme and continues to progress in leaps and bounds every minute of every day. For a multitude of reasons, more and more avid literary fans are opting to purchase e-books instead of paper books. The question from those not yet initiated into the world of electronic reading is simply: *Why?*

1. *Price.* An electronic title at Ellora's Cave Publishing and Cerridwen Press runs anywhere from 40% to 75% less than the cover price of the exact same title in paperback format. Why? Basic mathematics and cost. It is less expensive to publish an e-book (no paper and printing, no warehousing and shipping) than it is to publish a paperback, so the savings are passed along to the consumer.

2. *Space.* Running out of room in your house for your books? That is one worry you will never have with electronic books. For a low one-time cost, you can purchase a handheld device specifically designed for e-reading. Many e-readers have large, convenient screens for viewing. Better yet, hundreds of titles can be stored within your new library—on a single microchip. There are a variety of e-readers from different manufacturers. You can also read e-books on your PC or laptop computer. (Please note that Ellora's Cave does not endorse any specific brands.

You can check our websites at www.ellorascave.com or www.cerridwenpress.com for information we make available to new consumers.)

3. ***Mobility.*** Because your new e-library consists of only a microchip within a small, easily transportable e-reader, your entire cache of books can be taken with you wherever you go.

4. ***Personal Viewing Preferences.*** Are the words you are currently reading too small? Too large? Too... ANNOYING? Paperback books cannot be modified according to personal preferences, but e-books can.

5. ***Instant Gratification.*** Is it the middle of the night and all the bookstores near you are closed? Are you tired of waiting days, sometimes weeks, for bookstores to ship the novels you bought? Ellora's Cave Publishing sells instantaneous downloads twenty-four hours a day, seven days a week, every day of the year. Our webstore is never closed. Our e-book delivery system is 100% automated, meaning your order is filled as soon as you pay for it.

Those are a few of the top reasons why electronic books are replacing paperbacks for many avid readers.

As always, Ellora's Cave and Cerridwen Press welcome your questions and comments. We invite you to email us at Comments@ellorascave.com or write to us directly at Ellora's Cave Publishing Inc., 1056 Home Avenue, Akron, OH 44310-3502.

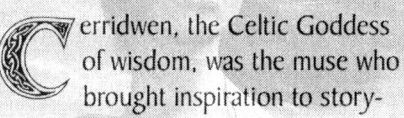

Cerridwen, the Celtic Goddess of wisdom, was the muse who brought inspiration to storytellers and those in the creative arts. Cerridwen Press encompasses the best and most innovative stories in all genres of today's fiction. Visit our site and discover the newest titles by talented authors who still get inspired - much like the ancient storytellers did, once upon a time.

Cerridwen Press
www.cerridwenpress.com

ELLORA'S CAVE
ROMANTICA PUBLISHING

Discover for yourself why readers can't get enough of the multiple award-winning publisher Ellora's Cave.

Whether you prefer e-books or paperbacks, be sure to visit EC on the web at www.ellorascave.com

for an erotic reading experience that will leave you breathless.